DES DILLON is an internationally acclaimed award-winning writer. Also a stand up comic, his novel *Me and Ma Gal* was shortlisted for the Saltire Society First Book of the Year Award and won the World Book Day 'We Are What We Read' poll for the novel that best describes Scotland today and was selected as one of *The List* / Scottish Book Trust's 100 All Time Best Scottish Books. His poetry and short stories have been anthologised internationally. His latest award was The Lion and Unicorn prize for the best of Irish and British literature in the Russian Language (2007). The Russian language version of his hit play *Six Black Candles* has been running in Kiev for a year and a new production by Goldfish Theatre – founded by Des in 2010 – is about to embark on an extensive tour of Scotland. He is the writer of the smash hit phenomenon of Scottish culture, *Singin I'm No a Billy He's a Tim*, probably the most-performed play in Scotland in the last five years. Des lives in Galloway.

Also by Des Dillon:

**Fiction**
*Me and Ma Gal* (1995)
*The Big Empty: A Collection of Short Stories* (1996)
*Duck* (1998)
*Itchycooblue* (1999)
*Return of the Busby Babes* (2000)
*Six Black Candles* (2002)
*The Blue Hen* (2004)
*The Glasgow Dragon* (2004)
*Singin I'm No A Billy He's A Tim* (2006)
*They Scream When You Kill Them* (2006)
*Monks* (2007)
*My Epileptic Lurcher* (2009)

**Poetry**
*Picking Brambles* (2003)

# An Experiment in Compassion

## DES DILLON

**Luath** Press Limited

EDINBURGH

www.luath.co.uk

First published 2011

ISBN: 978-1-906817-73-2

The publishers acknowledge the support of

towards the publication of this volume.

The paper used in this book is recyclable. It is made from low-chlorine pulps produced in a low-energy, low-emissions manner from renewable forests.

Printed and bound by
CPI Antony Rowe, Chippenham

Typeset in 11pt Frutiger by
3btype.com

# Last month

I remember what it was – we were off to buy another Bruce Springsteen album. I'd turned Joe onto The Boss. I was doing everything I could to make up for all the years I wasn't there. Me and him had made good progress this past wee while. It was good to be walking along the main street with my son and I was off to Barcelona that night with Penelope. She was ten years older than me but still beautiful inside and outside. I was going to Woolies closing down sale to pick up a few last-minute things.

Joe seen Billy Brown in the distance and nudged me.

—There's that guy Billy, said Joe.

I was trying to avoid him even though I'd heard he was back at the meetings. But before I could do anything Joe shouted him over.

—Billy!

That's when I seen he was steaming. He was two steps forward, another one forward for good luck and one to the side. Any side. Carrier bags pulling him down like anchors. The bus swerved onto the kerb to miss him as he staggered across. The bags swung out and hit me on the legs as his big red face shuffled its features. I realised I could've got away cos he was only beginning to recognise me.

—Aww! All right big fullah, he says so the whole main street turns round. He grabbed me and held onto me. He was stinking of Buckfast and pish. The bags hit me behind the knees and I could feel the lice jumping from his hair to mine.

—I heard you were off the drink Billy? Back at the meetings?

He un-hugged me and gave me a face between apology and defeat. Offered me a can of Super.
I was off it ten years but I didn't want to rub it in or put Billy down. He offered one to Joe. Joe just screwed his face up politely. I wanted away from there.

—They're doing Bruce Springsteen for a quid in Woolies, I said.

♫ I come from down in the valley, sang Billy. Loud. —where mister when you're young. They bring you up to do like your daddy done...

My body was leaning away in case he got to the chorus. But he stopped abruptly, holding one finger in front of his face.

—Your Danny's up the chinkee's close.

I looked at him with a big *what?* on my face.

—Danny and Shelly. This is our cargo. They're up the chinkee's close.

Shit! If I don't go up Billy'll say – seen your Stevie and his son on the main street. Danny'll ask if he told me he was there. Billy'll say aye and I'll be all the cunts. I didn't want to go up. Anything can happen up closes. Then I thought – ach! What's the harm in chewing the fat with my young brother for a couple of minutes? Up we go through the reverberation of our own footsteps. The light and sounds of the main street fading.

Shelly's a beached whale with dyed blonde hair. She's sitting on the wall and I swear the wall was bending underneath her. She's not right the lassie. She was pregnant for two and a half years once. Told my Maw and sisters she was two months and as time went by she kept on saying she was overdue, the doctor said it would definitely be in the next week.

—Anytime now Annie, she'd say to my Maw. It was hard to tell if she was pregnant or not so at first nobody was suspicious. But once she was twelve months we started to click. After that my Maw and sisters just humoured her. Is that right hen? Aw that's a sin. Can they not do anything for you? Bring you on? Something like that?

—I've to go in next week Annie, she'd say. — They're going to seduce me. But nobody laughed. It was a liberty to laugh at her.

—Look who's here! Billy says and Danny turns at an impossible angle. His scars were healing up nicely. His right arm is crooked out in front of him and a can of Super swings from his thumb and middle finger,

—Danny look who it is! Look who it is! Shelly's shouting.

—For what *hic* do we owe the honour! Danny says. —For what do we owe the honour! *Hic*.

He came and flung his arms round me. By this time Joe was pressed against the wall, watching. He'd slipped into a parallel universe without noticing. This one.

—Must be a special occasion. That's all I can say – must be a special occasion, Shelly's saying as Danny cries all over me.

Sobbing so much I could feel his chest pounding off mine and his back going up and down like a boned balloon. And d'you know what was going through my head? Not his tears. Cos you can never trust the tears of an alky. The only thing they're sincere about is where their next drink's coming from. What was going through my head was –
I hope he doesn't spill that beer on me. If he does I'll stink of alcohol. I'll have to walk along the main street. People'll smell it and think I'm back on the drink. In this town it'll only be a matter of hours before my Maw starts worrying about me all over again. But then I thought – he's an alcoholic, he's not going to spill a drop. He's got the can in a mechanically sound pivot between his thumb and middle finger. The beer stays parallel to gravity as the can goes every which way. So I let him cuddle me safe in the knowledge that he'd not spill a drop. In the background Shelly was still talking. I couldn't really hear at first cos Danny was shouting.

—Shut it you. This is my brother come to visit me. Keep your mouth shut!

But she keeps on going and that's when I hear what she's saying.

—I want a cuddle, Shelly sobs, —I want a cuddle.

At first I think she's taking the piss but when Danny breaks off to slap her in the face I see she's deadly serious. She does want a cuddle.

—What did I tell you? says Danny and slaps her. The slap echoes round the place. Its ring diminishing with the increasing pain.

—Fuck sake Danny, says Billy and pulls him back.

Danny punches Billy full force on the chest and Billy reels onto his arse looking up at me.

—Leave it Billy, I say. Billy nods okay.

—I only wanted a cuddle, Shelly says, —I was only asking him for a cuddle.

Danny lifts his hand again and I grab it. He was never very strong and I always was. So I pulled him gently back and went over to Shelly. I got down on the wall beside her. My hands couldn't even meet behind her. She grabbed me and locked her fingers at my back. Pulling. As if she was trying to pull herself right out of that miserable existence. I knew she'd been abused when she was young but now I could actually feel it. Nothing; not the smell of drink, nor the stink of tobacco, nor stale sweat, nor the waft of pish, could've stopped me giving her a cuddle. When I loosened my grip she held on tighter. I tried to let go but she squeezed.

—Don't let me go, she kept saying. —Don't let me go.

A tear came out of me then cos I knew there was no way she was ever going to break free. I decided to hold her for as long as it took. Bruce Springsteen would have to wait.

After a minute I heard Billy crying. Billy Brown. The best boxer in the west. A legend. Crying.

—What about me? he was saying. —What about me? I want a cuddle.

Shelly let me go.

—Give Billy a cuddle, she said, —Billy needs a cuddle.

He was over in the corner and his cheekbones were wet. I gave Joe a look as I passed him. I don't know if he ever knew what that look meant. But I tried to say – sometimes there's things in life you've got to do, Joe. Sometimes Joe, you've got to look over and beyond your prejudice and disgust and disappointment. Sometimes you've just got to love, Joe.

But I don't think he got all that.

I took Billy and held onto him. Man drowning at sea. Billy'd been sober a few times and we both knew what that meant. Some bit of him was trying to climb out. But it was all caving in. Tumbling.

—Everything's going to be all right Billy, I said, —everything's going to be all right.

But I knew, and Billy knew, and everybody up that close knew everything wasn't going to be alright. Everything was going to be far from alright. Billy pushed me away, looked in my eyes and said,

—You better get out of here big man. This close is no place for you.

—Don't you tell my brother what's good for him and what's not, Billy! Danny shouted.

—Don't hit him Billy, I whispered. —Not unless he hits you – then just do what's necessary.

Billy pulls a blade out. Waves it in the air making wee swishing noises by blowing air out of his mouth.

—I'll look after him Stevie, don't you worry.

Shelly starts shouting, —Billy's goanny kill them three bastards that chibbed Danny! Slash them to bits! Ain't ye Billy?

Billy looked me straight in the eye as he told her to shut her mouth. He kissed me on the cheek and everybody watched as I kissed him back. It was a moment of true love.

—Coming Joe? I said.

—Eh aye! He was and quick. Joe had that *what kind of a crazy place is this?* look on his face when we were walking out that close. Then a pique of guilt made me turn, go back in and thrust twenty quid in Danny's hand. He's going to get drink anyway and my figuring is the sooner he gets to where he can't take any more the better. Or maybe that's not it. Maybe that's me trying to moralise. To be the good guy. I think the truth of the twenty quid is more like this; I know what it's like to be choking for drink and have no money. Danny took the twenty and was crying. This time the tears were real. But they turned from despair to anxiety to anger to aggression and he went for me. Lunged in with a big haymaker of a punch. It was a postcard job. I could've made a cup of tea as I waited for it to come over. I dodged sideways. Billy held him back and Danny started ranting.

—Embarrassed to walk down the main street with your brother?

—What? I said.

—Embarrassed to walk down the main street with your brother?

—Nobody said nothing about walking down no main street Danny.

But he kept repeating himself so I said, —Come on then, we'll walk down to The Fountain and back.

He spat on me. That was his answer to that.

—I'm not walking down no fuckin main street so you can show off that you're sober! Oh look at me everybody! I've been off the drink for ninety years!

He swung a punch and hit the wall. Danced about sucking his knuckles.

—Look what you've made me do, he kept shouting. —Look what you've made me do!

There was no talking to him. I decided it would be best if I went. Joe was hanging about the edge not knowing to be embarrassed or not.

—I'm away, I said with no venom nor emotion that you could detect.

—See ye later, said Billy.

—Thanks for the cuddle, said Shelly. —Oh you've got lovely eyes by the way!

—It wasn't that when you were up this close with us ya prick! shouted Danny and ranted; bringing up the past.

—Shut up Danny! said Billy.

—He's an alky Joe – did ye know that about your Da? Eh? A dirty no good alky!

—Clamp it Danny, I'm warning ye! said Billy.

I was nearly back on main street when he shouted it.

—He killed a guy Joe, did ye know that?

Billy grabbed Danny but that didn't stop him.

—A punch. One punch Joe. He's a fuckin murderer.

Billy clamped his hand over Danny's mouth. But it was too late. The word echoed along the close and staggered out onto the street. People were walking in an arc round about it. Whether they knew it or not, they had heard it. And Joe had heard it. As I left the close I could hear their voices lessen. It reminded me of something I had read in a book about Romans. Echo was a nymph who was in love with Narcissus. But when he didn't love her back she pined away till only her voice remained. Only now I couldn't tell if it was Danny pining away or me.

Out on the main street the sun was shining and people came and went about their business. Joe sighed the way you do at a blinding movie. Like the opening scene of *Saving Private Ryan* or Rutger Hauer's speech on the roof in *Blade Runner*, or when Oedipus sticks thon pins in his eyes when the guilt for fuckin his mother finally hits home. And I was thinking about how easily we can pollute our whole family, our whole society, by the things we do, when Joe spoke.

—Come on Da, we'll go and get that CD, he said. It was the first he'd ever called me Da. Joe never knew what I'd been in jail for but he never mentioned *murderer*. Not then and not since. We were lucky. We got the last copy of *The River* and I raved about it all the way back to the car. He got in just before me and I took a second to look at him and say a prayer or make a wish or whatever it is I do – that he'd not end up in the darkness of some close breaking his whole family's heart. We droove off and at The Fountain I could see, in the distance, the chinkee's close like a black hole in the brightness of the street. I watched it in my wing mirror till it disappeared into a dot and wondered if I'd ever see my brother again. Joe turned up the volume and The Boss sang loud and clear.

♫ Now those memories come back to haunt me, they haunt me like a curse. Is a dream a lie if it don't come true, or is it something worse, that sends me down to the river, though I know the river is dry…

# New Year 1986

I came shuffling downstairs New Year's Day with my eyes half-shut against bright light and a cunt of a hangover. The smell of booze and stale smoke and that post-party silence.

Monastic.

Except this slight movement. Like a cat. Or a mouse. There was two unopened cans of lager at the bottom of the stairs. But the last thing I wanted was a drink. I went in the scullery and filled a pint tumbler with water. Downed it in two. Breathed out a long alcohol-laced sigh, traces of whisky on the back of my tongue, filled the glass and went to inspect the carnage in the living room.

It was the aftermath of Troy. Bodies lying on the floor. My Da near the fire with a pizza of vomit for company and a few uncles, one with a burst lip, another with a lady's dress on. And Danny balanced on the corner of the couch with a half-full tumbler of McEwan's Export. Flat. He tilted his head from side to side and laughed. At that time he had these big Joe Nineties with thick black rims and an elastoplast over one lens to train his squint into alignment.

—What's that you've got?

He took another slug and held it in the air. Started singing,

♫ McEwan's is the best buy, the best buy, the best buy, McEwan's is the best buy – the best buy in beer.

He went *hic!* and fell sideways off the couch. This disembodied chant came up.

—Hey! McEwan's! The best buy in beer!

Then the empty tumbler rose on the end of an arm like Excalibur. When he stood up he was staggering everywhere. He fell on top of my uncle Peter who snorted and shouted.

—Celtic! Mon McClair!

I tried to waken my Da but he rolled over and lay like a dead man. When I turned back Danny was wrenching a glued-on whisky glass from the table. He downed it in one and said, —Ahh! Like he's seen us all do many's a time. Then he gave us 'Bonnie Wee Jeannie McColl'.

♫ A fine wee lass, a bonnie wee lass, is bonnie wee Jeannie McColl. I met her at a wedding at…

And he stood there cos he couldn't remember where he'd met bonnie wee Jeannie McCall. I started laughing. He was funny. This miniature drunk man. It kinda highlighted how fuckin stupid we all look on the drink.

—The cooperative hall Danny, I said, —I met her at a wedding at the cooperative hall.

He sang on.

♫ Met her at the dancing in the cooperative hall!

Then, with two hands, he twisted another glass free. As he drank it and smacked his lips, I shot up the stairs and woke my Maw.

—Maw, Maw! Danny's steaming, I shouted. — Pished out his head so he is. Down the stairs.

She sat up not knowing quite where she was. There was two other aunties on the bed and they sat up with hair like a witch's in the wind.

—What? she said.

—Danny, he's down the stairs and he's steaming, I said. —Drinking all the dregs.

Danny was the baby so she was up like a ten bob rocket, beating me down into the living room. Danny was back on his perch waving his latest glass in the air and singing 'Ten Guitars'.

My uncle Paul, without even looking up, threw a shoe at Danny. Danny dodged, pointed and said, — Ahh haa!

—One singer, one song! shouted Peter in his sleep.

—What's that you've got son? said my Maw.

♫ Whisky for my daddy o dum a doo dum a die, sung Danny and fell off his perch.

My Maw ran over and grabbed him. He was all floppy now and doing a mixture of 'Ten Guitars' and 'Don't Go Breaking My Heart'. My Maw dragged him over to my Da.

—Matt, Matt! she was shouting.

My Da sat bolt upright.

—Time's it?

—Eleven, I shouted.

—Peter, get up, my Da said. —We'll miss the game.

—Look at the state of him! my Maw said.

My Da looked at Danny. Danny's one-eyed face stared back with a massive grin.

—Awright Matthew? said Danny.

—Has he been drinking?

—Drinking? Look! she said. And she let Danny go. He slid to the floor in instalments and lay face down like a starfish. Singing.

♫ Oh you're drunk you're drunk ya silly old cunt as drunk as you can be...

My Da laughed. Woke Peter and Paul.

—Hey – look at this.

But my Maw wasn't laughing. She was worried. She handed me some tens.

—Run down and phone an ambulance! she said.

Three busted phone boxes later I phoned nine nine nine. Danny got rushed up the hospital and got his stomach pumped. I went an all with my Maw and Da. The doctors didn't have much to say. Their attitude said it all. They thought we'd been feeding Danny drink all night such was his alcohol count. That he'd joined in with the Hogmanay party with the adults.

—But is he going to be okay? asked my Maw.

He was. My Da managed to wangle his way to the game. I went home and crashed a can and sat in my room smiling at Danny and his 'Ten Guitars'. Fixing

the story right in my head for telling that night when
I went round the parties burning like pagan fires all
over that dark new January.

# Winter 1998

It was half eight and my Da'd not arrived so I decided to go out and lay the pans along the ring beam. There was a few inches of hard packed snow topped with ice and the whole site had a blue glow. Here and there Liam Brown's labourers huddled near fires with their arms wrapped round themselves. But we were on a price so the shutters had to go up. And anyway, the concrete was coming in the morning. Once you order you've got to pay for it. The gaffer had already asked where my Da was and I said not to worry.

By half nine he'd still not arrived. I'd managed to erect some of the ring beam myself but you need two for setting the bolts. I went back to the hut at ten. Liam wanted to know where my Da was. I just shrugged and said he must've been on the drink. But he wasn't asking out of concern. Him and his squad of Irishmen got a bonus per cubic metres of concrete and if the shutters didn't go up they couldn't pour.

As I sat and read the paper, glancing now and then to see if my Da's car had arrived yet, the hut filled with men with nothing to do. It was like a sauna steaming with old sweat and rancid wellies, donkey jackets and oil skins swung on nails. Men munched their pieces. Some drank from secret bottles and some drank openly. Now and then one would ask *where's your Da the day then?* Thinking about it now reminds me of Penelope's house. All they greedy fat bastards waiting about, scoffing Odysseus's grub and booze. Not caring a fuck for anycunt but themselves. Well, it was the eighties, a time when everycunt wanted it all for themselves. And we're still not over it yet.

Then in he came behind a breath of cloudy air.

—Aye Matt! they were saying. —Later the day.

—On the drink last night, my Da said. He had a black eye and his hand was bandaged up. I looked at him and so did the rest of the hut. But nobody asked. I was about to ask when there was Danny behind him. And Danny had a right good black eye an all. The hut turned back to murmuring. None of their business. But they were listening. They could talk about one subject and listen to another no problem.

—Happened to your hand? I said.

—Ach that wee cunt attacked me.

—He attacked me! said Danny.

The hut took a quick breath and my Da silenced Danny with a look. Held his bandaged hand up in the air. It was a white trophy in the middle of that hut. It was a kind of announcement my Da made. So that nobody would need to ask again.

—I broke this punching him. So I've brung him to hammer in the nails.

There was a quiet from the workers and they started filtering out. They didn't discuss what had just happened till the other side of the site. My Da threw Danny an old nail bag and hammer. Danny put it on. He was a picture stood there with that old nail bag and the hammer dragging it down. A gunslinger with the wrong belt.

—Get a cup of tea and meet me out there, said my Da and went out to see what had to be done for tomorrow's concrete.

Danny watched till he was halfway across the site talking to the gaffer, then, instead of tea, he produced a can of Super from nowhere.

—That's a good trick, I said, —do that again.

And he laughed. And he did. He done it again. Chucked me a can from somewhere on his skinny frame. I downed it, crushed the can and sent it spinning like a silver bird out over the canal. It skidded on the ice and slid to a halt near the pointed corner of an iceberged Asda trolley. Danny crushed his and dropped it in Liam Brown's welly. That was us started. We drank all week after that. I was more of a bout drinker whereas he drank all the time. His whole life was drinking and my whole life was trying not to.

—What the fuck happened Danny? I said.

And he told me the story.

My Da'd tried all the ways since Danny was eleven to stop him drinking but none of it worked. Talking. Laughing. Drinking with him. Battering him. Not battering him. Taking him to the pub to teach him to drink socially. Telling him stories of family members destroyed by drink. Alcohol was killing everybody. It was like a machine gun where the bullets come out yearly but endlessly. His uncle looked great at forty-five. Wife left him. Five years later he was eighty-five. I was with my Da this day when he seen this uncle sitting on the packie's wall. Shaking like Parkinson's disease. My Da sat at one side, I sat at the other. Gerry looked at my Da. Hung his head and sighed.

—Don't give me the lecture Matt, is all he said.

So my Da talked to him about the old days for a while. And to me, the youngster that I was at the time, the old days sounded great. I mind when we walked away my Da saying, —See that son, that's what drink does to ye.

Three weeks later Gerry was dead.

—It's a good job Catholics don't cremate, my Da said, —he'd explode, Gerry! Soon as they flicked the switch.

Eventually my Da washed his hands of Danny and his drinking. So Danny would come home drunk every night, talk shite and -slabber and go to bed. But if Danny came in drunk and my Da was drunk; my Da'd go for him. They'd end up fighting and my

Da always won. But last night, Danny says, he landed
a cracker on my Da just before the arguing started.
Pre-emptive strike. My Da fell back and tripped over
the chair. Danny managed to get a few into him and
was riding on the glory of his first win when the bold
Matt regained his senses and shoved Danny back.

—Come on then! Danny says, —D'ye want more of
that?

And he showed me how he held his fist in the air
like a club. Like a warning. But Matt lunged forwards
and caught him such a crack he broke his own hand.
Danny said when he came to my Da had his right
hand in a basin of cold water and a whisky in his
left hand.

—You're coming to work with me in the morning,
he said. —I can't hammer so much as a fuckin nail in
so you're going to do it for me.

And he'd forgot all about this, Danny, until he was
dragged out his bed this morning.

—With his left hand of course, Danny said and
laughed.

On the way up Danny had to change gears cos my
Da was holding the wheel with his left hand.

—Yees coming out or yees staying here all fuckin
day? my Da says when he poked his head back into
the hut.

We walked with the gaffer to the ring beam. He
kept looking at Danny. A skinny rake of an eighteen-
year-old, the shaft of his hammer almost touching

the ground. I could tell my Da had told him the story of how Danny was here to hammer in the nails.
As my Da talked to the gaffer about wee changes in the bolt positioning I filled Danny in on what we were doing.

—We're building a rectangle of concrete, I said, — and every now and then a big box of concrete. In the box go the bolts, sticking up into the air. When we're finished the steel erectors come and bolt the steel columns and beams on.

Give him his due, Danny, he got it in one. Understood what it was all about. Me and him had them pans up in no time and my Da got the theodolite and we set the bolts. By mid afternoon we were finished. Bolts set to less than half a mil. Level as Loch Lomond. Liam Brown was impressed. His one eye was going left to right and sparkling more than it might if he had two.

—He's a rare wee grafter that Danny fulla Matt, says Liam Brown.

—Aye, when he's sober, says my Da.

He didn't know Danny and me'd been boozing all day.

On the way back to the hut Danny asked what were we building anyway? I told him it was an MFI.

—What, them that leaves the nuts and bolts out the kitchen units?

—The very cunts, I said.

—Mmm, said Danny and stroked his chin, —MFI?

In the hut you could feel my Da was still angry at Danny. He took two painkillers, stared at him then ordered him out to get rid of the cones from yesterday's pour. Of course Danny didn't know what the fuck the cones were so I went out.

I handed him a gallon of petrol. The bolts are wrapped in an upside-down polystyrene cone. When the concrete sets we get rid of the cones and then the bolt is free to move in a wee circle. Gives the steel erectors a bit of leeway. Danny shook his head. Produced another can from nowhere and set off along the ring beam. I went in and rolled a fag. My Da wasn't much for the crack so I said nothing. He sat there looking at the drawings. Working out how the changes were going to fit in.

After ten minutes Liam Brown came in laughing. His big red ex-boxer's face wiped with a smile.

—Have yourself a look out there, he said.

We went out and all along the ring beam was rows of flames. Like Olympic flames. Black smoke rising into the cold blue day. Danny was at the head of these flames and he'd bend down, pour four helpings of petrol then lean back, fling a match and whoosh up they'd go. He moved on to the next row. We were all at the hut laughing (except my Da), when the gaffer ran screaming across the park.

—You don't light them, the petrol melts them, he was shouting, —The petrol melts them, you don't need to fucking light them.

Danny stood up looking back along the line of flames. For a second he didn't know what to do then he ran along the beam trying to stamp them out. Of course the bits of polystyrene stuck to his feet and there he was, his feet on fire, running along this beam like that prick Icarus. His Da, Daedalus, built wings of wood and feathers stuck thegether with wax so that him and Icarus could fly away from this island they were trapped on. Daedalus warned Icarus not to fly too close to the sun. But Icarus dickarus flew too close and the wax melted. Icarus fell into the sea and drowned.

I looked round and my Da was shaking his head and laughing.

But Danny had the last laugh, secret though it was. The next day Liam Brown and his men were all over the next set of bolts, pouring concrete down the sides of the pans and everywhere they shouldn't. We worked like fuck alongside, re-positioning the bolts when the big boghoppers stamped on them. Cleaning as much of the spillage from the side of the pans as we could. By twelve it was all over and we retired to the hut.

Mid afternoon, as we were setting up the next section of the ring beam, the gaffer let out a scream. He'd been looking through his theodolite checking the bolts but when he got to the last set they weren't there. The board and all the hangers were there. But the four bolts had been unscrewed and removed just before the pour. And now the concrete was set. He came running over to us.

—Where's the bolts? There are four fucking bolts missing.

—They were there just before the pour, says my Da. —Sure did you not check them yourself?

And he had to admit he did, the gaffer. He didn't know how it happened. He called for Liam Brown and a jackhammer and as they drilled Danny came over and gave me a secret slug of Buckie.

—MFI, Danny said. —See how they cunts like it. When they've got fuckin bolts missing.

We laughed. But nobody knew what we were laughing at.

# October thirteenth 2002

From a distance it was obvious Shelly was asking folks for money. It was only when my Maw got closer she noticed the flowers. Shelly had them close to her chest and fag ash was falling onto the heads. It was one of them wee bunches you get outside Asda for two quid.

—Hi yi hen.

—Oh hi yi Annie, Shelly said.

—What's the flowers for hen?

—For Danny boy Annie.

—For Danny? His birthday's not till Tuesday.

—I know but I love him, Annie, she said, —I pure love him so I do.

And my Maw knew that must be true cos even if Shelly paid fifty pence for these dog-eared flowers; that was fifty pence further from a bottle of White Lightning. My Maw looked about but Danny was nowhere to be seen. Shelly told her he was in bed with the flu. That meant he'd be hiding up some close with a case of the horrors. Probably watching.

—Any loose? Shelly asked a passing ned.

—No Shell. Not cashed my book yet.

That embarrassed my Maw enough to give her a fiver. Shelly thanked her and was about to head for Haddows when my Maw stopped her.

—Tell Danny to meet me outside Asda at six on Tuesday. I'll give him his birthday present.

—Right Annie, Shelly said but she wasn't listening so my Maw wrote a note and stuck it in Shelly's pocket. And all the time, my Maw told me, she could feel Shelly's gravity tugging in the direction of the off-licence. Her whole body drifting for drink, every molecule twisted. When she let her go my Maw swears she moved the first three yards in a quantum blink.

The note said;

*Dear Danny. Meet me outside Asda's at six o' clock on Tuesday night. I'll bring your birthday present.*

*Love, Mum*

It was a tradition that had built up this past ten years because Danny spent most of his time on the main street drunk, or sleeping up closes. My Maw would meet him on his birthday and give him his present, which was always a good pair of boots, a pair of really tough trousers, a jacket mountaineers would be proud of and fifty quid for drink.

When she was in the café my Maw watched Shelly come out of Haddows with a carrier bag and go up the chinkee's close. By the time she'd finished her tea and had a smoke Danny and Shelly were out. She was going to go and remind Danny when she seen him reading the note. He stood there crying then stuffed it in the pocket of last year's jacket, took a long slug of White Lightning and wandered off arguing with Shelly about something.

Ten to six on the Tuesday my Maw was outside
Asda. It was October thirteenth. A Friday. Black
Friday. Danny's birthday. And even though it had
been warm in the morning the wind had got up and
my Maw was getting chilly. She could've went and
stood under the heaters in Asda but she didn't want
to miss him. If he came and didn't see her he might
go away feeling sorry for himself. Alkies were PhDs
in the poor mes. She stood shivering and thought
about when she had him. Her ninth wane. And big
complications. Serious medical stuff. Touch and go.
She'd nearly died. It was October and it was raining
and it was 1980. Outside the window was all her
wanes and Matt. And she felt, and Matt felt, that
it was the last time they'd see each other. She died
twice, my Maw. First time it was a long white tunnel
with angels singing hymns she said. Then next time
Our Lady was floating in the corner. In a sky blue and
radiating light, no, love; that's what it was, a love
that looked like light. Or a light that looked like love.

—Am I dead Our Lady? she asked and Our Lady
shook her head no.

Days passed. Next thing she remembers was a cry.
They'd brung Danny from intensive care in his
incubator. He was small and shrivelled and looked
like he wouldn't last the night. And… Jesus what
time is it!?

She looked over at Brennan's clock and it was just
after six. No Danny. He'd only been premature once
in his life. She smiled, my Maw, at her own patter.

A few people came and went and spoke about this and that and before she knew it, it was seven.
The bags got heavy and she had to put them down.
She started asking people if they'd seen Danny.
But nobody had. Not today anyway. They had stories about him from other days. Stories my Maw didn't want to hear but they had to tell. She listened with a quiet smile of despair.

She was certain he'd turn up. Not for the clothes. He'd be there for the money. The money was a Trojan horse. The procedure was this: he turned up, she gave him the bags of new clothes, he went into Asda toilets and changed, gave my Maw the old ones. That's when she'd give him his card. He opens it and hands Shelly the fifty quid. He'd stand talking till Shelly came back from Haddows, he'd kiss my Maw, tell her he loved her, and off he'd go. But my Maw, she loved Danny more than he loved drink – and that's going some hurt. My Maw'd go home then and wash the old clothes, sew and fix them up any way she could. She'd get the boots re-soled and take a taxi to leave the bundle outside Shelly's house. Cos they spent their time near the money and the drink up main street you could never be sure when they were home.

By eight o clock my Maw was worried. He'd always turned up before even if Shelly had to carry him. Cos even if an alky's drunk he leaves some brain cells spare for where tomorrow's drink is coming from.

He wasn't coming.

She whispered *Happy birthday Danny* and walked away fighting back tears, the wind bouncing the bag off her bad knee.

On the Thursday Danny was outside Asda at four o clock. The drink he'd had that morning was wearing away and he was rubbing his palms over and over. As if he was trying to absolve himself from something. He could feel the shakes coming and Shelly was wandering about asking for loose.

—Just to keep us ticking over till Danny's Maw comes, she told everybody.

Danny had shoplifted a bar of soap from Boots cos he didn't like the soap in Asda toilets. He was looking forward to the new gear but mostly the fifty quid. He tried to remember what age he was. He was late twenties. But was he thirty yet? All he knew was; this is Thursday the thirteenth. This is my birthday. My wee Maw always meets me on my birthday. Outside Asda at six o clock. She always gives me fifty quid, I put on the new clothes, she gives me the money.

Shelly was on good form. By five she'd managed to get people to feel sorry for her to the right degree without being disgusted and begged two bottles of cider. By six there was no sign of my Maw. Shelly was drunk now and putting people off. They were giving her a wide berth.

By seven Danny's mouth was dry and Maw didn't look like she was coming. Fuck it. There was nothing for it. He decided to go into Asda and lift a couple of cans.

Security picked him up soon as he walked in. They were twenty feet when he got to the drink section. Danny spotted them so he wound back to the door and lifted a basket. Shelly joined him and they waltzed about like a shopping couple, except they stuck out like a couple of refugees. Security followed. Now and then they went to the drink aisle.

It was a stand-off.

Danny and Shelly wanted that booze but there was two security guards between them and it. Danny lifted four cans of Super, put them in the basket beside the beans and expensive beauty products and walked away. It was hard to believe Shelly'd been beautiful in her teens but pregnant at fifteen started her on the slippery slope to Uglyville.

When Danny lifted a can of ratatouille and launched it into the drink aisle, the crash of glass sent the security running. What they thought when they seen a can of ratatouille among smashed wine bottles is anybody's guess but they're quick and they soon realised Danny had something to do with it. They ran along, heads twisted up the aisles. But no Danny. No Shelly. As they searched the supermarket Danny and Shelly were down the fire escape steps in the damp concrete basement guzzling the Super. They downed one each in seconds and Danny stamped the cans with his year-old boots, flattened them and slid them out under the fire escape door.

The fire escape had a glass lock that broke when you opened the door, setting the alarm off. They took their time with the other two cans. Danny gave them the same treatment and posted them out, with some Pringles, to the seagulls.

Security was surprised to see them again at the drinks aisle still holding four cans of Super.

—Right come on Danny – out.

—He's waiting on his mother, Shelly shouted.

—Aye – that's right, I'm waiting on my mother. It's my birthday.

—Happy birthday Danny, but I'm going to have to ask you to leave.

—What for? I'm shopping. You can't fling me out if I'm only shopping. That's discrimination that so it is.

—We're not flinging you out. It's eight o' clock. We're closing.

—I don't care, I'm not leaving!

The big one got Danny by the arm but Danny wrenched free and ran. Who knows why he ran at that moment. Maybe he was caught up in the whole mother thing, some warped family pride. Things go on and off in a drunk's mind like fireworks, making them victims of their own unpredictable thoughts. That's what I was like anyway. And in some way Danny's actions seem perfectly normal to me. I can identify.

Anyway – Danny ran and security followed. He slid and fell turning at the chickens, the guards were almost on him when he launched a three pounder. They dove behind the beans and Danny threw five chickens in quick succession. It was like Baghdad. The last people at the checkouts were craning their necks to see. You can't make this stuff up.

—I'm meeting my mother, Danny was screaming, —it's my fuckin birthday!

And another frozen chicken crashed into the beans. Give these guards their due, they started launching tins of eleven pence beans at Danny. He was out in the open, Danny, and as he raised a chicken above his head a tin caught him on the shoulder and spun him round. He fell and they were on him, pinning him to the floor. By now Danny was crying his eyes out shouting for his Maw.

—Mammy! Mammy – where are ye? Where are ye Mammy?

One guard had Danny's wrists and the other had his feet as they carried him wriggling and yelling towards the checkout. But they never counted on the bold Shelly.

—Tommy! the wee one with the moustache shouted, but it was too late. Shelly clunked Tommy with a turkey and down he went. Danny got away running on all fours like it was a skating rink before getting upright and making for the door, where two big cops grabbed him.

—Leave him. He's waiting on his mammy, Shelly said.

Danny struggled and spat and sank the teeth in.

The cops wrestled him to the ground and locked him all fancy with cuffs in jig time and as they steered him away towards the cop station, security caught up.

—She hit me with a turkey!

—What!?

—Look at that, said the guard, showing the cops his head, —she hit me with a turkey. I want her lifted!

The cops turned to Shelly. —Did you hit him with a turkey?

—They were flinging the cheap beans at us!

—And he was flinging chickens! said the guard with the moustache.

The cops couldn't hold it in any longer and burst out laughing at the same time.

—That's assault that, the guard was saying, —I want her lifted!

Shelly kept herself out of arm's reach and the cops weren't for letting go of Danny to catch her. They tried to convince the guard they'd lift her later, she wasn't going more than a hundred yards of Haddows, but the guard wanted her lifted now. His head was bleeding and a big lump was appearing.

—That was a sixteen pound turkey, he said, —d'ye want me to go and get it as evidence?

As the cops and security argued Danny, despite the cuffs, got his fingers locked into the middle of a long line of sleeping Asda trolleys and the cops jerked to a halt. They tried to tug him free. The guards joined in but Danny screamed so loud a crowd gathered, shouting to leave him alone. It could turn ugly, the cops said, and told security to back off but try as they might the cops couldn't work his fingers loose.

—My Maw's coming here with my birthday present, Danny ranted, foaming at the mouth. — Nocunt's going to stop me meeting my Maw, he said, —Nocunt. Nocunt!

He shouted that last *nocunt* like a war cry. Like Mel Gibson shouting *Freedom!* The cops set about prizing his fingers loose. One at a time.

—Argh! Argh – you're breaking my fingers, Danny screamed, —help – they're breaking my fingers.

The crowd surged forwards. Chanting Danny's name. Cos they all knew him. He was alky-in-residence.

—Daa-nay! Daa-nay! Daa-nay!

It was *Dog Day Afternoon* outside Asda. Every time the cops even looked at Danny's fingers he screamed and the crowd booed and jeered. Chanted his name with Shelly conducting while in the background the guard still ranted about the turkey.

—I'm waiting on my Maw, Danny shouted sideways to the crowd, cos he was horizontal. The cops thinking if they hold his feet in the air long enough his hands'll weaken and he'll fall off.

—It's my birthday, he shouted and the crowd stated singing.

♫ Happy birthday to you, happy birthday to you, happy birthday dear Danny, happy birthday to you.

Even the cops joined in. And Shelly milked the situation for loose. Danny was bubbling and crying now.

—My Mammy's meeting me here for my birthday, he saidwith saliva running down his chin, foaming with that enormous pride you get defending family traditions. A big snotter bubble was expanding out of his nose. And to the degree that snotter bubble repulses you is the degree to which you lack empathy.

There's our stalemate.

Eventually one of the cops had an idea.

—Get twenty pound coins! he said to his mate.

—Eh? Pound coins?

—Look, one two three four five dad a dad a da… twenty!

—What?

—A pound for each trolley, free him and we'll wheel him to the station.

The other cop got the coins and they slotted them into the Asda trolleys until Danny drifted free. There was applause from the crowd and the clever cop took a bow. But Danny wasn't letting go so they dragged him away by the feet. The boos rose over the rattle of the trolley and Shelly ran along behind it shouting.

—No, don't lift him. It's his birthday. Ye can't lift him. I pure love him so I do. I can't live without him. Dannny!

# Winter 1998

I let Danny down the last of the Buckie before
we got out the car. *Nebraska* was playing. It was
'My Father's House' and The Boss was on good form
with his religious metaphors and fuckin existential
dread done better than all your philosophers. And
shining though all that his humanity. It made me
want to cry. The Boss could accept anybody for who
they were.

—You ready? Danny said and brung me back to
reality.

It was a big plush building with nothing to
associate it with concrete excepting if you knew the
name. Sterling.

It was a babe that was inside. Long legs out under
her skirt and the stockings rubbed off each other as
she turned in her chair – sending electricity everywhere. She smelled like happiness. Didn't take more
than a glance at us. With our gear covered in
concrete and a few days' growth we were a pair
of ugly cunts. The drinking wasn't helping either.
Our faces blotchy red and our eyes had took on that
mad look. She made us wait a few moments then
asked how she could help us in a tone of disgust. Or
something else. What was it now? Something like
ascendancy.

—We're here to see mister Sterling.

—And you are?

—The Dolan brothers.

When I said it I knew we sounded like a cowboy movie. She hung her head to grin and searched some sheet of paper.

—You don't seem to have an appointment.

I just stared. Danny copied me. In our padded tartan shirts we looked like a couple of hillbillies. Brothers obviously, him skinnier and a foot taller. We eventually unnerved her.

—Do you have an appointment?

—It's about the money we've been docked.

She looked blank at that.

—I'm sorry, mister Sterling can't see you without an appointment.

But she made a mistake because, as she said *mister Sterling* she glanced at this big mahogany door with all sorts of brass furniture on it. If it wasn't construction I'd swear it was a funeral directors.

—Do you wish to make an appointment? she said. Which meant *would you please get to fuck out of here.*

—Mon Danny, I said.

As we walked away I felt her grin stabbing me repeatedly in the back but we swerved and opened Sterling's door before she could squeak and had it snibbed before she arrived, banging on the mahogany shouting all about the cops.

Got to give Sterling his due. Kept his cool, looked up and said,—Yes? Can I help you?

He looked like somebody in a movie about the devil. Or Zeus – when he's trying to act cool dishing out advice to Athena when she's fuckin about with Odysseus's life. And who were these cunts to be messing about with people's lives? Who the fuck gives them the authority?

—Can I help you?

There my head was away again.

—I want my money, I said.

—And you are?

—We're the Dolans.

Fuck it! We sounded like a cowboy movie again. Stirling made his eyebrows ask for more information.

—We're doing the shuttering, the ring beams, on the MFI job.

—Mm mm, he went like a doctor.

—We've been ripped off and we want our money.

—Take a seat, he said, sweeping his arm over the expanse of teak table. Danny complied with an obedience to posh accents that's bred into us by fathers, teachers and mothers.

—I'll stand, I said and walked towards him. It was a long walk.

A

Long

Walk.

I stood there trying to intimidate him but he never flinched.

—I want my money.

—I can't give you *your money* as you put it until I know exactly what *money* you're speaking about.

He's like a fuckin lawyer now. I told him about Liam Brown's squad pouring concrete all over the outside of the pans and how we cleaned some of it but it was their job to clean the rest and how I had to use a JCB to break the pans out and Sterling i.e. *him* had docked five hundred quid off my money.

—If you damage plant you have to pay for it, he said.

—Aye, but I only damaged it cos Liam Brown's squad left the concrete on them.

—Nonetheless, those pans are your responsibility.

—And the fuckin concrete is Brown's responsibility.

Danny seen the flash of anger in my eyes. It was coming up. I was fuckin volcanic. The lid the lid. Keep the lid on.

—Look pal, I said, —take a step back, the ethics of the thing are clear. Brown's bad workmanship forced us to take an action that inadvertently,

but not deliberately, damaged the pans. He was knowingly negligent. I had a bit of bad luck.

At first he looked surprised by the clarity of that argument and if he showed any fear in that office that day, it was at them few sentences.

—As I said, he eventually said, —those pans are your responsibility.

The argument went round and round. I kept

blaming that one-eyed bastard Brown and Sterling kept blaming me.

—Right. Right! I said with my hands in the air. Conversation fuckin terminated. Finito. Kaput.

He leaned back and motioned us to go but I had other ideas.

—If you don't give us the money I'm going to wreck this office.

And just to show him I meant business I lifted a sheaf of important papers and flung them all over the place. They came down like giant confetti. The secretary with the sizzling stockings was still banging on the door. There was another bigger, tougher bang too.

—Security, said Sterling and I'm sure I heard a hissing before he closed his mouth.

—Security, I said, —fuckin security?

By now poor Danny was chalk white.

—Right. That's it!

I lifted a chair and crashed it off the door. In the silence that followed we heard:

—Mister Sterling, are you okay?

—I'm fine, he shouted and I wanted to shake his hand for his coolness but I was on a mission. I was focused. I lifted another chair.

—This one's going right out the window, I said. — Then I'm wrecking the whole place.

—I'll call the police.

I slid his phone over.

—Phone them, I said, —here. I'll dial the fuckin

number. And as soon as you hang up I'll smash this joint up – thenI'll smash you up.

By this time I had him by the neck. But he still didn't lose his cool. He simply flipped a chequebook open and lifted a pen. I let go.

—How much?

—Five hundred and seventy-five, I said.

He wrote the cheque. There wasn't a trace of tremor in his writing. Handed it to me.

—This better not bounce, I said.

—It certainly won't.

I nodded to Danny and we went to the door. When I opened it the sexy secretary and this fat security guard stumbled in. He grabbed me.

—Hands off, I said, pressing my face right into his so he could feel the moist anger of my spittle, see the bulbous rage of close-up eyes.

— Midway this way of life we're bound upon, I snarled, — I woke to find myself in a dark wood, where the right road was wholly lost and gone.

That was one I remembered from school. The guard stepped back. I could see the terror in his eyes. Everything is a weapon, in the right hands, at the right time. I turned before we left and said,

—I suppose that's me sacked off the MFI job?

—No. I'm happy for you to finish that.

—I suppose that's me fucked for any more work with Stirling then?

—Not if your price is right, he said.

And d'you know what? I believed him. We droove

straight to Stirling's own bank and cashed the cheque there and then. Woke up the next morning in my flat surrounded by empty bottles of booze.

# Autumn 2008

The evening before my release I was looking out the cell, smoking. Two eagles were over the hills to the north of Perth. They turned on each other, fighting and falling hundreds of feet before one broke off and flew away. My cell mate said it was a bad omen. It set the butterflies loose in me and I couldn't sleep all night. My life was going through my head and in the morning I didn't look like a guy about be released. Sof met me at the gatehouse and gave me a wee parcel of books.

—To keep you going, he said.

The light outside a jail is different from the light inside, it loses something behind that perimeter fence. And I was the right side of it for the first time in seven years wondering if anybody was watching from their cells. That's when I seen Danny the other end of the car park. Even though he hadn't visited this past two years he came. It brought a lump to my throat and I walked towards him smiling. Closer. I knew by his blank face he didn't recognise me. Closer. Seen the reason he'd stopped visiting. Drink was really taking its toll now. I knew that anyway. Even though my Maw and Da and sisters kept saying he was too sick to come. Or that it broke his heart to see me in the jail. But stories filtered through. Stories

about him and stories about Billy. Stories go everywhere. Stories are unstoppable. The truth always gets
through.

When he did recognise me he started crying cos
the jail sucks up everything you are. I was crying an
all. He thought his crying had set me off but I wasn't
prepared for how much the booze had ravaged him.
He managed a smile against the run of his face.

—Taa naa! he said and produced a carry-out from
nowhere but the old tricks were now meaningless.

I hugged him. The carrier bag crackled like the
fires of hell.

—All right? I said.

—Aye, he said back.

It's funny how inarticulate we are at the biggest
moments of our lives. We can write the lines in later.
Or make them up before. But somehow they never
come out in the moment but maybe we don't need
them anyhow. We hugged for as long as it took –
patting each other on the back, cars going past on
the main road, shift change screws heading for their
families and the big red stripe of Tesco advertising
the march of everyday life.

When we broke free he opened a bottle of
Buckie and held it out on the end of a smile.
The sickly sweet waft of that thick liquid poured
into my nostrils and a hundred Buckfast nights
came back.

—Get this down your neck big man, he said.

—No Danny.

He laughed and motioned his arm up in a short sharp beat.

—Mon, he said.

—Haven't had a drink for seven years.

—Well I know that don't I! he said, grinning like a clown. —You've been in the fuckin pokey! Not unless you've been on the exploding plastic bottles.

He took my hand and wrapped it round the bottle, pushing it towards my mouth. I pushed it back.

—No Danny – I meant I've been going to AA meetings in the jail. I wrote and told you that sure!

—Aye but I thought you were just going for a fag and a sandwich. Something to do. Here, take a swig.

—I'm on the programme, Danny!

—Programme? he said and spat on the sunlight. —You're not an alky, ye just got into a fight when ye were drunk!

I never answered him. I gave him the Buckie back.

—Ach fuckin take a drink.

I shook my head.

—Suit yourself then, he said and started slugging.

He'd finished that bottle by the time we got to the station. We fell out on the train because I wouldn't take a drink of the next bottle and by the time we got home he was gibbering about Liam Brown's funeral. How he got drunk and went. Stood at the back. Mother of Christ they were singing, star of the sea. Danny was singing pray for the wanderer, pray for me when they seen him and flung him out.

I had to get away from him and he had to get away from me. There's nothing worse than being on a bender and some sober cunt.

When we parted I went and sat at the canal, chipping stones and watching the ripples. Maybe I was just Danny's excuse that day for a drink. It was nothing to do with meeting his brother out the jail. It was just the drink. I got to thinking about my life and the things I'd done. What I had left of value. Got to thinking about Joe.

I missed Joe in jail. Me and his mother split up when he was two and the more I drank the less I seen him. I seen him once in the year before I went to jail and not at all the past seven years. That was one of the things my AA sponsor advised me to do, try to rekindle the relationship. I started with letters. Told him a lot of things in them letters. Told him I was only a boy when I left. Told him I was an alcoholic. Told him I didn't really leave cos I didn't know where I was in the universe anyhow. Or where I was going. I just kinda floated away. Into the cold. Told him I done him and his mother a favour, considering the way my life went after that but I wanted to make up for it now. Make some kind of amends.

The letters he sent back never mentioned the things I'd wrote. Maybe he was embarrassed. I didn't question it. I just keep sending my deepest feelings and he'd send back a list of what he'd been up to of late. But he did reply. Every time. And it was good getting a letter from Joe. I could sit it there for days before opening it. Savouring the anticipation. My cell mate thought I was crazy.

—Ye goanny open the fuckin thing?

It was his letter an all.

I got a slap-up feed at my Maw's. My Da offering me drink the same way Danny had done.

—Jesus Christ Da, I said, —if I got offered this amount of booze for free when I was on the drink I'd've been pished every day.

—You were, he said and we laughed.

Can you not get our Danny to go to that AA thing? my Maw said.

I said I would try.

I went and met Joe at seven. It was pre-arranged in my last letter but I wasn't sure if he'd turn up and I got quite a shock when I seen him. He was a giant. Six feet odds and good-looking. It took me a while to equate this boy with the baby I left behind. All my years I'd rocked a bundle of guilt in my arms. I'd need a crane to lift this one.

—All right Stevie? he said.

I knew he couldn't bring himself to call me Da.

I was taking the first tentative steps. I tried to talk about the important things but he kept talking about music. So I started talking about music too. That took us on a different course, sailing for his heart.

# Three weeks ago

Three weeks ago Shelly was on her own on the wee bench outside Asda.

—Where's Danny the day hen? my Maw says.

—I don't know Annie.

—Ye don't know?

Sometimes Danny slopes off following a carry-out. His figuring is that they might accept one but two have got no chance. He tells Shelly to wait for him. Don't move. And she does wait. She waited twenty hours one time. Used Asda's toilet.

—Well if ye see him tell him I'm in Mackays, My Maw said, —I'll be up here another hour.

When she came back out of Mackays Shelly called her over.

—I know where he is Annie.

She took my Maw up the chinkee's close. There was Danny snoring in the sun with his top off, sun-burnt down one side. When my Maw woke him he couldn't tell if he was fifteen and waking up on the scullery floor with a hangover, or thirty and waking up in the July sun.

—What did I tell you Shell!

And he swung a boot at her.

—Here you! said my Maw. —Leave that lassie alone or I'll buckin boot you.

—He telt me not to disturb him Annie.

Danny got up and attacked Shelly. They had each other by the hair spinning around shouting.

—Let go.

—No you let go first, ya hoor.

—No you let go.

My Maw stuffed a tenner in Danny's pocket as it spun past and left the close.

That was three weeks ago. Nobody'd seen hide nor hair of them since. My Maw asked me to go and search. See if I could find Billy Brown. There'd been reports of him going about. I looked at her.

—I'm worried sick son, she said.

So I agreed to look for Billy. When I was in jail and I heard what happened to him I couldn't believe it and when I first seen him after I got out he was a wreck. I avoided him. Kept my distance. If I seen Danny and Shelly on their own I'd talk to them but if Billy was there I'd do a donnybrook. But there had to come a time when we'd be face to face. My sponsor said I can't keep running, or disguising my fears as some kind of morality. When I faced up to them they'd fizzle away.

I asked Joe if he fancied a bit of detective work and he did. He wanted to talk anyway about *Nebraska*. When I picked him up I seen my ex glaring from the window. I didn't resent her though. How could she know the changes I'd gone through? The work I'd done on myself? As we droove away I told Joe all about Danny going missing and my Maw

being worried sick and me on the hunt for Billy
Brown. If we find Billy we might find Danny.

—What does he look like? said Joe.

—A right jakie, Joe. If you see any dirty smelly
tramps gimme a shout.

We droove through the streets of that town, me
wishing the bubble we were in was the extent of our
universe, that nothing outside it, not space nor time
existed, that we were a father and son with the right
kind of history.

—What about *Nebraska*? I said.

—Man, Da, that's one sex-offender of an album.
Wooh!

—Liked it then?

—Liked it? I've got it here.

He shoved it in and ranted about it.

—Springsteen done it for the white trash, he said.
—He's our poet, The Boss. No pretence whatsoever.
Like Dylan?

I agreed and we listened. And we joined in. We
were starting to have things in common, me and Joe.

Joe sang along with State Trooper.

—Packed with emotion, I said.

—And it means the same here as it does in
America, Joe said.

—The lost and the fuckin lonely, I said, —That's
who the Brucie boy likes. Them that live in the
darkness on the edge of town.

And we listened till Joe turned it down to release
an idea.

—Communism right? Communism tried to connect something that was already connected. All round the world it was already connected. Poverty.

He was at uni now and I was glad he was jettisoning himself from this stinking culture.

—But Springsteen's made the connection, he said. —He's a working class God! I bet middle class cunts think it's all shallow. They can't see the depth cos they don't know nothing about the life. There's more humanity in that one album than the complete works of Shakespeare. And the only thing holding academia back from seeing it is a lack of education, ignorance masquerading as snobbery.

I praised Joe. I'd never thought about it but he was right. From one angle we were the great dismissed. But from this angle, the Bruce Springsteen angle, it was them, the snobs; they were the great dismissed, they were The Excluded.

We never found Billy and I was secretly glad about that. At the cop station the desk sergeant knew Danny really well. He was on the night he got lifted out Asda. The two cops had brought him in dragging an Asda trolley. The whole station was on a high that night. Stuff like that made his job worthwhile.

—But when did you last see him? I said. —Was it in the past three weeks?

—The walk, he said. —The Orange Walk.

—Danny was at the Orange Walk? Is he a proddie now?

—At the walk – aye. Part of the walk – no! Aw he's some kiddie that brother of yours, this cop said and proceeded to tell us how Danny got lifted for his own good. —He came running up that street there with a thousand Orangemen behind him. Came right in here and vaulted the desk. Lock me up. Lock me up, he was shouting. He'd been skipping along drunk bursting the orange balloons with a pin.

Me and Joe had a laugh at that with this desk sergeant and he promised if he got a sniff of Danny he'd phone my Maw's number. We thanked him and left.

We went round to my Maw's for tea. None of the sisters had found anything out, no hospitals had anybody like that, no jails. They even tried the monasteries. Then Dina remembered Danny asked the doctor for rehab in Castle Craig. The doctor had promised him a place soon. That was nearly a year ago but maybe it had came up out the blue. My Maw grabbed the phone book but when she called they were sorry. They can't give out personal information. The doctors were the same.

Then I remembered this guy. Posh John. He was at our meeting last week and he said he helped out at Castle Craig. I phoned a couple of AA punters and got Posh John's number.

But he'd not seen anybody like Danny in Castle Craig. My Maw was starting to think he was dead, that they were going to turn up his body in the canal. But Jean pointed out that the two of them were missing, Shelly and Danny, it was unlikely the two of them died at the same time.

—What if they committed suicide? said my Maw.
—A pact?

—Don't be so fuckin daft, Dina said.

There was silence then a look of horror came over my Maw's face.

—Oh Jesus, she said.

—What? I said.

—Oh Jesus Mary and Joseph!

—What is it Mammy? said Dina.

—What if that Billy Brown's murdered the two of them?

—Billy Brown couldn't pull the leg off a roast chicken. He's finished, my Da said.

—Danny stole his wife off him! my Maw said.

And although we all tried to convince her she was havering there was that wee bit in everybody's head that said hey – maybe Billy did kill them, maybe they're buried in a shallow grave. I decided I'd find Billy just to put my Maw at ease.

By midnight I was about to give up when I saw him in the doorway of the Pound Shop eating a fish supper. I parked up the road and walked back, kidded on I was surprised to see him.

—Billy!
—Stevie!

And he held out the fish supper. It was nerves really. I had a lump of hot fish in my mouth before I seen his bogging nails and dirt-ingrained hands. He offered a bit to Joe but Joe's brain was working better than mine.

—Eh, no thanks, he said.

—How long's that you're out now? Billy said.

—Three months.

—Still sober?

—Seven years now.

He shook my hand on that one.

—Not seen ye about? said Billy.

—Aye. Keeping a low profile.

—Danny and Shelly keep bumping into you but.

I said nothing. He knew I'd been avoiding him.

—Did ye hear what happened to me? he said.

—Aye.

—Everything?

—Aye.

—You've heard everything?

I looked him straight in the eye so he knew I was telling the truth.

—I've heard everything Billy. Guy sent down from Peterhead told me.

And at that Billy started crying. He held his arms out. I hugged him and he hugged me. We held on. And it was like we were holding on to a bit of our past, a spot away back behind all our troubles, a time when we never realised how happy we all were.

He pulled back, looked me in the eyes and said,

—Thanks.

—Billy, my Maw's worried sick about Danny. Him and Shelly's went missing.

Billy nearly choked on his fish, laughing.

—Went missing!? Have they fuck!

—She thinks you've done them in and buried them in a shallow grave. Or not so shallow in Shelly's case.

He laughed again.

—They're away on holiday, he said.

—Where?

—Saltcoats. They're in a caravan down there.

He gave me a bit of paper with the address and the caravan number. Told me they cashed their books down there. I thanked him and walked away.

—Stevie? he shouted.

I turned. —Aye?

—Don't ignore me the next time you see me eh?

I nodded my head. —I won't Billy.

When I phoned my Maw I thought she'd be relieved. But she wouldn't believe a word that came out that Billy Brown's mouth. She wanted me to drive her to Saltcoats. Joe went an all. We played *Nebraska* and Maw hated it.

—Get that off, she said. —That's buckin suicide music. No wonder there's so many young people committing suicide these days if that's what they're listening to. Have ye no happy music?

I stuck in The Dubliners and she sung all the way to Saltcoats.

♫ Her eyes they shone like diamonds. They called her the queen of the land...

The caravan site it was massive. And even though

Billy gave us the row and the number we didn't need it, cos it was two in the morning and there was this almighty racket coming from one. We snuck up. There was Danny, a cider bottle in one hand and his arm outstretched pointing at Shelly, shouting something we couldn't make out. My Maw watched for a minute, cried for another minute then asked me to take her home. I asked did she not want to go in and see him? But she just wanted to go home, she was tired. I felt sorry for my wee Maw then. She was all wore out. She hardly touched a drop in her life yet drink was killing her. We could still hear Danny and Shelly fighting when we got back to the car.

# 2008

Danny turned up in a hell of a state this day, greeting and snottering and wanting off the drink. Living with a bird and her ex-husband when they were all alkies was doing his nut in. Shelly fell out with Danny and he hit her a slap. When he woke in the middle of the night she was in the spare room with Billy by way of revenge. It wasn't the first time Danny had arrived at my flat wanting off the drink but usually, as soon as he woke up, he was offski.

I made the couch up as a bed and I was surprised in the morning when he still wanted to go to AA even though he was shaking and choking for a drink. There was a meeting in the community centre at eleven so I sent him for a shower and gave him some of my clothes. When he came down he looked much better, till you looked into his eyes that was, then you knew here was a guy suffering.

At the meeting they gave him half-cups of tea and advice in one ear and out the other. He was crying all the way through and when they asked if he wanted to say anything he shook his head. I thought there was no hope for him. We went to another meeting that night and when we got home I told him he goes back on the drink he's out. Truth be told, I thought it would be days.

But a week later he was still sober and my Maw was pleased and her eyes a happy blue. She came round every day and cooked us dinner. And she'd sit there till it was about seven o clock, quarter past.

—Right off yees go to your meeting now, she'd say, —I'll tidy up.

She'd fix Danny's jacket and hair, licking her hand and patting it down like she done when we were kids. Give us money for fags and tell us how proud she was. Her two sons sober and shining like pins.

— Our Blessed Lady be thanked, she'd say, —I can walk up that buckin street with my head held high now.

A week after that we seen Billy and Shelly outside Asda. They said hello and Danny nodded back. But he was gutted and in Asda some invisible force started dragged him towards the drink. I got him out of there and into a meeting. When it came round to him he burst out crying and went on about how he loved Shelly and it was breaking his heart. Progress had been made.

—My name's Danny and I'm an alcoholic, he'd say.

But there's nothing in that. It's harder not to say that when everybody else is saying it. But he started talking about his past. When he told them he started drinking at six a few of them tutted and sneered like he was exaggerating. But he wasn't. When it came round the room to me I let them know about finding him drunk that New Year's morning. The room had a right laugh at that story.

Three months later, to everybody's surprise, Danny

was still sober and still away from Shelly. He was getting his old sense of humour back. We had a laugh about the old days. The time him and Billy turned up to steal the fireplace and I ended up stealing it for them to get some fuckin peace.

About that time this woman had started going about the meetings. She was about ten years older than me. Dark hair, alright dyed, but still dark. Nice brown skin, beautiful eyes. I couldn't be certain but sometimes I caught her looking at me. She had a posh accent and I thought, no! what would a woman like that be doing looking at me? Maybe it was because I was forever looking at her. Apart from her being a babe, I felt I knew her from somewhere but couldn't figure out where. I listened for her name when it went round the hall.

—Hi. I'm Penelope and I'm an alcoholic.

Penelope, I said over and over in my head. Pen el oh pee. Pen e lope. Penelope. Hi Penelope I'm Parker. No. No – hi Penelope. Then I realised she was Odysseus' wife. Hi Penelope – I'm Odysseus. I *am* Odysseus. Big-headed prick that he is. Although you can't help liking the guy for his patter. I realised I was staring when she smiled and gave me this tiny wave that I couldn't decide to resent or not.

One night, before the meeting started, she sat next to me and Danny. Started chatting.

—Good meeting this, she said.

—Aye. I froze, but she chatted on. All AA stuff.

—I think I know you from somewhere, I eventually said.

—Funny, I was thinking the same thing.

She said it with such music that I didn't know if she meant it literally or if she was the same as me. That is – falling in love.

—I've seen both of you before, she said.

Boof! My dream fizzled out. She looked at me and looked at Danny.

—Where have I seen you? she puzzled.

—Ever been pished up the chinkee's close? Danny said.

—Hardly, she said, giving Danny a little push and laughing, more patronising herself than us. I tried to join in but my words weren't working.

The next week she came in with a bright face. Straight up to me and Danny.

—Let me see your arm.

She pushed Danny's sleeve up. There was the big scar.

—My signature, she said, and traced her finger round the scar. I looked at her and realised it was the beautiful doctor who sewed him up.

—And those, she pointed to my eyes, —they were either stunningly beautiful – or wildly insane.

—Insane, I said.

—Oh I don't know.

She held my gaze and my heart punched my lungs so that I couldn't breathe.

—And the fact – that week my husband had just run off with his cousin.

—That was about nine years ago?

—The start of my downfall, she said and motioned drinking.

The bell went for the meeting and I sat down. Beside her. In love. Hoping she was too. All through that meeting I wanted to grab her hand and hold it. It was millimetres away. There was an electrical storm between us nobody else could see. I knew she was waiting for me to make a move but rejection paralysed me. Her being a doctor wasn't helping much either.

Me and Danny arrived at the community centre the next week early. I could see the old place had an effect on Danny. He'd practically been brought up there.

When he was five my Maw got a job in that community centre. He'd go there after school and the school holidays. Video games were just coming out. Breakout, Space Invader, Galaxian; nothing had the beating of Danny – his was the first computer-generated childhood. He got a chicken supper every night. Came out in a rash. Nobody knew what it was till he seen a specialist. Turned out to be a chicken rash. We called him Chicken George for a few years after that.

—Hey Chicken George! I shouted and Danny smiled. He seemed glad I remembered and I got back to setting out rows of chairs. Danny filled the urn and put it on.

—Where's the teapots and the cups an all that? he shouted.

—In one of them metal cupboards over there.

I was finishing the last row when I heard a gasp. I turned and there was Danny two paces back from this cupboard, staring.

—Stevie! he said as if Liam Brown's ghost was in there. He was shaking but it wasn't Liam Brown's ghost. It was rows and rows of whisky and vodka and rum and all sorts of fancy wine.

—Look at that, he said, his eyes were wide. — Look!

It was treasure. Somebody was having a party that week. A wedding or an engagement. I don't know what Danny was thinking but I thought it was like the bag Aeolus gave Odysseus with the three winds trapped in it. Only the west wind is left free to blow him safely home but his sailors think Odysseus is hiding treasure and they open it. The fury of the three winds blows them away from Ithaca in a right cunt of a storm. Away from home. And we're all being blown safely home in AA, unless somebody opens the bag.

—Shut the fuckin door! I said in panic. But Danny was still ogling the booze.

I banged it shut.

—Here gimme a hand, I said.

Me and Danny lifted a heavy table and wedged it against the door.

—Tell nobody, I said.

—D'you think I'm daft?

—Aye, I said. —Sometimes.

I meant it and he knew I meant it.

I sat through that big meeting feeling a low drone from that cupboard. Some punters looked over as if they'd seen something, then they looked away. People were asking if I was okay.

—Aye, I'm just worried about our Danny, I said.

—Och, he's doing great, they said. —Day at a time, they said.

I got my sponsor in a quiet corner and told him about the drink. He didn't seem that bothered. A lot of punters own pubs. He was right. I hadn't thought of that. I told him Danny was mesmerised when he opened that cupboard. My sponsor said keep an eye on him but if he does slip that was nobody's choice but his own, no matter how hard it was to accept; this was the truth of the matter.

In the morning Danny wasn't there. His blankets were neatly folded over the couch. They made me think of shrouds. I heard the community centre got screwed. I heard Danny, Shelly and Billy had one helluva party. Danny knew that place like the back of his hand. He would have been in and out in minutes.

I went to a meeting that night and they asked me to do the table. I'd done tables before but I was panicking. Penelope was there. With her shifts she sometimes missed for a week and I hadn't seen her since Danny went back on the drink. I was sure once she heard me talking about why I was in the jail she'd go off me. She gave me a wee wave and a smile as the meeting started.

—My name's Stevie and I'm an alcoholic...

Even though I shared where the booze took me and didn't miss out on the jail and all that had happened, I went on mostly about Danny being back on the drink cos that's where my head was that night. When I was finished and punters were shaking my hand Penelope came up and kissed my cheek.

—Well done. That was great, she said, —I found it really uplifting and I feel I know you a bit better.

She gave me a hug. That's when I blurted it out.

—D'you want to go out on a date? I said. About ten people heard it too and they smiled and waited on the answer.

—I thought I was going to have to get that out of you with invasive surgery, she said and gave my hand a wee squeeze.

My sponsor winked.

# 2006 sometime

About a year before my release I got a letter off
Libby. About this party my Maw had. It made me
laugh and it made me cry. I passed it round the jail.
It was one of the sisters' birthdays or whatever.
They'd enough of men getting drunk and fighting so
they invited only women; contacted all the aunts and
female cousins. But my Maw had a gut feeling she'd
left somebody out and they all sat there trying to
puzzle it, going over and over the lists.

—Shelly! my Maw eventually said.

—Shelly? said Jean. —Danny's bird?

The sisters looked at my Maw like she was mental.

—She's part of the family, my Maw said.

—They're just drinking partners, said Winnie.

—Sure did I not meet her the other month there
with a bunch of flowers for him. What are they for
hen, I said. For Danny boy Annie, she went. I pure
love him. How's that just a drinking partner?

And none of the girls could argue with that. Next
day, outside Asda, my Maw asked Shelly to come to
the party.

—Can I Annie? Can I really? I'd love that so I
would.

But Danny was reluctant to let her go. Same as he
was reluctant to let my Maw go. That was half of his

problem, he'd never had to fend for himself, never came to realise his life was his own responsibility. Danny asked my Maw if he could come.

—It's all women, she said.

He took the huff and my Maw promised to give him twenty if he let Shelly come.

—Gimme it the now well, he said.

—When you bring that lassie to my door.

Night of the party Danny turned up with Shelly. Billy was standing at the end of the street. My Maw gave Danny twenty and off he went to get drunk with Billy. What my Maw was thinking at that time was; did Shelly walk across the town wearing that dress? The party was buzzing when Shelly walked in. All the women kept talking but the volume went down and nobody was really listening. They were amazed at Shelly in this white dress three sizes too small. Bingo wings and things. She had been a babe when she was younger but that was hard to see now as rolls of fat made the dress look like a wad of dough.

—That's a nice dress, said Dina.

Shelly spun round but the dress never flared out as it must've done years before.

—I'm going to wear it when me and Danny get married, she said.

—Yous're getting married? said Winnie.

—Mm mm.

—When's that hen? says my Maw.

—Soon as we have the baby, said Shelly patting her belly.

—How long's that you're pregnant now Shelly?
Libby said.

—I don't know, she said, looking at her belly.
—Ages.

—Two fuckin years! Jean said to Avril.

—Sit over here, said Libby.

They sat her down and acted as normal as they
could. Shelly had her hands on her lap looking round
with lifted eyebrows and a closed-mouth smile and
people smiled back in much the same way.

—What do you want to drink hen? said my Maw.

—Any Buckie? she said.

They thought she wasn't serious but she was. A
few of them stifled their laughter.

—We forgot to get the Buckie, says my Maw.
Some of the posher aunties are horrified.

—Any cider then?

Luckily they had cider. The conversation sped up
again and beneath that women where asking who
Shelly was. It was Danny's bird. She was an alky. She
was at least two years pregnant now. She wasn't
right the lassie. A right Walter Mitty. Starved of
oxygen at birth. Used to be beautiful, they say. It's
a pure sin for her so it is.

When they had a good drink in them Libby started
asking Shelly questions. All they knew about her was
this past few years with Danny and a bunch of
rumours about her past.

—So how did you and Danny meet? said Libby.

—Met him outside Asda.

—Outside Asda, that's great hen, said my Maw.

—Billy knew him, said Shelly.

—Was it love at first sight? said Carol.

—Aye. Mm mm. He's got lovely eyes.

The girls looked at each other cos Danny had a squint.

—So have you got any wanes? said Jean.

—Seven counting this one, she said and patted her belly.

Avril passed on a *she's nuts* sign to the woman who believed Shelly had seven wanes. Nobody could recall ever seeing her with a wane.

—Is that not a long time to be pregnant? Libby said.

But my Maw shooshed her.

—Seven for god sakes Shelly, said my Maw, — you're nearly as bad as me.

—Where are they the night? Jean asked. —Is your mother watching them for you?

—My mother's dead.

—Oh I'm sorry. You must miss her hen.

—No.

A gasp from the women.

—You don't miss your poor dead mother, says my Maw.

—She died having me.

—Who's watching your wanes then? said Jean. —Your Da?

There was a strange lost look from Shelly before she answered.

—They don't stay with me, my wanes, she finally said.

—Where do they stay then? said a baffled Carol.

—They're in care.

And she said that like you'd be telling somebody the milk was in the fridge.

—In care? Avril says. —They took them off you?

—Aye. They took them off me.

The only change in her voice is that her vowels were slowing right down.

—What for? says Libby.

—Cos of Billy. Mm mm, cos of him.

—Billy? asked Avril.

—With him being a beast an that.

—A beast? says my Maw. —Does he batter you hen?

—No, she says. —A beast!

Even though she said it louder none of them knew what a beast was, so she told them.

—Billy's a feedofile, she said.

—Billy Brown's not a paedophile, said Dina. —He was a boxer!

—He is, said Shelly, —that's how they won't let us keep our wanes. Soon as I have this one they're taking it off me.

—You shouldn't go making things like that up hen. It can get people into a lot of trouble.

—He does Annie, she said. —He tampers with wanes. That's how he was in jail before he met me.

—Billy Brown was in jail for police assault, Avril said.

—Aye that's when he tells everybody. I'm glad I've got Danny. Danny's good to me. Aye he's not a beast. Not Danny. They'd let me keep it if it was just Danny. Billy's a beast but.

And drunk now she rocked back and forth repeating *Billy's a beast* into the silence of that room. All the women in disbelief, passing sly sighs and glances.

—Right, says my Maw, clapping her hands to break the curse, —who's first to sing?

Nobody. So my Maw sang 'Carrickfergus'. Then Sadie done 'The Mountains of Mourne'. Winnie done 'Perfect'. Only every time she sung *perfect* Shelly shouted *Asda*.

—It's got to be ee ee – Asda!

That started everybody laughing. They even joined in singing *it's got to be Asda*. In the midst of all that my Maw asked Shelly to get up and sing. She protested but they pushed her up. She could hardly stand the poor lassie and she was a sight in that Pillsbury-doughboy outfit. She went red and tried to sit again but no matter where she went they buffeted her back up. Then they started stamping and chanting *sing sing sing*.

♫ Shelly, Shelly give us a song, give us a song…

Clapping and clicking glasses off the table. They didn't hear Shelly start deep underneath their chants, but they saw her face change. Suddenly she was an angel, her head tilted and her eyes gazing up. She was that sincere, half the women looked to see what she was looking at. By then silence had fallen and her voice was like crystal singing:

♫ So fare thee well my bonnie lass,
    so deep in love am I,
    and I will love thee still, my dear,
    till aw the sea gan dry.

    Till aw the seas gan dry my dear,
    till aw the sea gan dry,
    and I will love thee still, my dear,
    till all the seas gan dry.

By fuck could she sing. And her voice resonated through that room so you thought glasses would shatter. They couldn't believe it. By the end everybody was crying and they all went up and hugged her one at a time, every last woman in that place.

Then who came into the living room but Danny and Billy. The women stared at Billy.

—What? he said.

But they stared.

—Okay so I've had a wee drink. So what? Coming home Shelly?

She nodded yes. Danny got hold of her. Gave her a wee kiss.

—Mon Shelly, he said. —We've got ye a bottle of cider.

Danny and Billy knew there was something funny in that room. They couldn't get out quick enough even though the place was awash with booze.

When they waved Shelly out into the night the women felt something wrench from their souls. But try as they might they couldn't figure out what it was. Avril was next to sing. And she sang it loud and she sang it clear. 'Send in the Clowns' it was. But nobody was laughing at the clowns. Nobody laughed.

# 2007

I'd put a bit of weight on since I got out the jail and all my clothes were too tight. Instead of drinking I'd took up eating. I was a fat bastard. Extra large. I bought a load of new ones out Asda. George it's called, the make. Kitted myself right out; socks, boxers, trousers, t-shirts, jumpers, shoes and a jacket and I packed my old gear in black bags for Danny. Figured him and Billy could always use a changes of clothes. I wasn't sure how they'd take me arriving round but that's not what mattered, what mattered, said my sponsor, was motivation. Whether or not I was genuinely moved to an act of charity. To the degree that was true is the degree to which my actions were genuine, he said.

—There's many ways to make amends, he said. —A few bags of clothes are nothing really. But you going round there with them? With the right motivation. That's spiritual, he said. —Pure fuckin spiritual.

I never knew exactly where Shelly's house was. I knew it was Greenend but didn't even know the street, so I went round and asked my Maw. My Da was shouting through from the living room.

—Up a close up the main street. He lives up a fuckin close!

My Maw closed over the door and whispered that it was a top right in Calypso Crescent. I could still hear my Da mumbling in the background. By this time, as far as he was concerned, Danny was *persona non grata*.

—It's a lovely wee flat, my Maw said. —That lassie keeps it nice and clean.

—Have you been in it?

—No, she says, —but I've seen it from the outside. It's got lovely blinds so it has.

Before I left my Maw had a look on her face. I knew she wanted to say something.

—What is it Maw?

—You know Danny's staying with Billy Brown and his wife? she said.

—Aye.

My Maw just nodded.

—So long as you know, she said, —it's a bit of a bad set up if you ask me.

I drew up outside the door. Top right. It looked like a house where the occupants have been on holiday for a long time. I humped the bin bags to the door with the whole scheme watching from windows. Probably thinking, here's a guy flung out. Moving in. I lifted the letter box and let it fall a few times. Nothing. Waited. Chapped the door quiet. Nothing. Chapped it louder. Nothing. Lifted the letter box. Nothing, except a bad smell. A right rotten smell. I started worrying about dead bodies. Maybe Danny was dead? It could happen easy with the demon drink. An argument, a fight, next thing somebody's dead. I imagined Danny lying on the floor in there somewhere. Or Billy. Or Shelly. Or any combination. Them all even?

I hammered that door. Shouted through, —Danny! Billy! Shelly!

But there was nothing. I listened without brea-thing and couldn't even sense movement. Then I heard this faint kinda hissing sound. Gas, I thought, fuckin gas. I sniffed the letter box. It didn't smell like gas. But maybe with the dead bodies and the gas – you never know.

—You alright?

It was the downstairs neighbour, short skirt, bare legs, black vest top and dark hair. Obviously been a bit of a babe in her time but scheme life had worn her down. Her body was still there but her face had gave up.

—Looking for my brother, I said.

—Billy? she said like she was surprised Billy had a brother.

—No. Danny.

—Aw. They'll be up at Asda's. They're always up at Asda's.

And she stretched showing off the sinews of her body.

—I was up there earlier, I said. —They've not been there for a few days.

She leaned back and looked up at the windows.

—I've not even heard them moving about, she said.

—Listen, I said, —don't want to sound morbid nor nothing but I think I can smell gas. Maybe...

She burst out laughing. I could see her fillings and she had good tits. What I was doing thinking about tits when my brother could be lying dead I don't know.

—Gas, she said, —fuckin gas – are you mental? There's no fuckin gas in there. There's no gas in this whole scheme. We're all electric.

—D'you like them, she said.

—Who?

—These, she said, holding her tits up with her hands and jiggling them at me.

—Pretty good, I said. —Are they both your own?

—Every kissable inch, she said. —D'you want to come into my house and wait for your brother?

I wanted to. I really wanted to. I'd not been very lucky on the woman front since I got out of jail. When I'd been on the drink I could get a bird but sober I didn't have the bottle to chat them up.

—My man's in jail, she said and kept my gaze.

—I need to find my brother.

—Suit yourself then, she said and walked away. She had a nice arse an all.

—D'you like my arse? she said and turned and smiled at her door.

—Any time, she said. —Remember that, any way you like it an all.

And in she went. So there was me at my brother's door. A stench seeping out his letter box. Three bin

bags. A hard-on and a head full of AA morality.
Up every skirt there's a slip. Especially a bit of
married skirt. I positioned one of the bags in front
of my dick and walked back to the car.

A window opened above me. It was Billy.

—Stevie!

—Billy! I said, unsure if I'd be welcome. But he
smiled and waved.

—Come on up. I'll let you in.

He opened a few locks and slid a few chains.
I hands him the bags mumbling something about
the clothes being good ones and I hope he's not
offended. He sounded genuinely pleased to see me.
He shouted up as he re-locked the door.

—It's your Stevie!

It was dark in there. He took one of the bags and
led me up the stairs.

—We never answer the door, he said. —Too para.
Know the score.

I did. Know the score.

Billy was struggling going up the stairs with one
bin bag full of clothes. When I breathed in I felt the
stench on every part of my mouth and my tongue
coating with something unpleasant. There was
another smell making it worse. Food. Frying food.
Me and Billy were rising into the thick of it. I put
effort into not being sick.

Top of the steps was a toilet that used to be white
but now it was yellow. Hadn't been cleaned for years.
Smelled like a public toilet in the 1960s, minus any

disinfectant or open window. I averted my gaze and followed Billy up the lobby. I could hear sizzling and realised that's what the hissing noise was. The scullery was a tangled mess of tins and bins and slimy things. It was as if somebody had dumped the contents of ten bin bags on every surface. But there was something else. A warm smell that traced through all the others. What the fuck was that? There it was. An oven tray full of sizzling chicken like rows of cooked little people, brown and the fat spitting off them. They were obviously about to eat before I turned up.

It was dark in the living room. The curtains were shut. Well, not curtains – it was two bed sheets hung over a pole. Danny was standing with his bottle of cider and one hand out ready to shake.

—You always liked chicken, I said, as we shook hands.

Then we fell into a hug holding back our crying.

—We were just about to have our dinner, Danny said. —Want some?

—No. I just popped in, I said. —I brung some clothes up. I'm too fat for them now.

Danny and Billy searched through the bags trying things on. By now the sweat was running out of me. Even though it was late summer and still hot, they had the heating turned up, the fire on full blast and all the windows shut. I think they were so dehydrated with alcohol that they'd stopped sweating. They were drinking a big plastic bottle of cider each. There was some empty ones flattened on the floor and two carrier bags with some new ones warming in the heat.

—Have a seat, said this voice.

It was Shelly. She was lying next to the fire on a mattress on the floor. Her blonde hair floating in the gloom. What I could see of her skin was corned beef and her mascara was a Hammer House of Horrors movie.

—Sit on the couch, she said.

I did. I nearly broke my arse and my knees smacked me on the chin. It was one of them couches where the stuffing has disappeared. They all laughed at me.

—That always happens, said Billy.

—Well no fuckin wonder, I said, —the stuffing's gone!

Even though they were top class jakies I felt like a schoolboy on that couch.

—How d'you like that? said Billy, wearing an old leather jacket of mine.

—I can't see it right Billy, I said. —Too dark in here.

—Open the curtains, said Shelly.

Danny tugged the blankets and they fell. Everybody screwed their eyes up but my sight returned long before theirs cos they'd been like ferrets for days.

Billy was in some state. One side of his face was black and purple and swoll up, two of his teeth were snapped.

—What the fuck happened to you Billy? I said.

—Don't tell him Billy, Shelly said.

—Three guys attacked me, said Billy, staring at Shelly.

—What for?

—Says I was a paedo and went for me.

—Aye, c'mere you ya feedofile bastard they shouted and came running over, said Shelly.
—Pushed me on my arse.

—What did you do, Danny?

—What did I do?

Danny showed me his knuckles. They were all tore and cut, some big splits filled now with dirt.

—I was laying into them win't I Shelly?

—He was, Shelly said, propped up on one elbow like a sex goddess. But try as I might I couldn't picture Danny laying into anybody, not unless they were comatose. He'd never had the bottle for stand up fights, even though he caused plenty. His mouth was always too big for his fists.

I tried to find out who these three guys were. My sponsor said if I wanted to stay sober I had to lose that protection mentality, or else my past would just drag me down. But ideas like that are easier to hear than absorb. Danny was my brother and I felt like I owed Billy. I asked all sorts of questions. They'd seen these guys about but didn't know who they were. Billy says they'd handle it themselves. No need to get involved.

—Anyway, d'you want to end up back in the nick? Billy says.

I gave up. I looked at my watch.

—It's half seven, need to go, I said.

—How – got an AA meeting to go to? Danny sneered.

—Shut up you, said Shelly.

—We're proud of ye big man, said Billy.

He came over and hugged me.

—Fuckin proud of ye.

Billy stood back. Looked at Danny.

Danny came over and hugged me but said nothing. I could understand. I'd left him far behind and he felt abandoned. Billy came down to lock the door. At the bottom of the stairs he seemed sober.

—You're in some state Billy, I said.

—Ach, he said and shrugged. —Hey – you better get to your meeting.

Outside I heard all the locks and chains going on. The neighbour was at her window. I looked straight at her and she looked straight back. When I got to the car Billy, Shelly and Danny were waving at the window. Smiling and waving. I knew I'd be the subject that night, maybe even the cause of a fight. I had one last look at them – framed there like a photo they couldn't escape.

I droove away with classic FM on, through that rougher than the roughest of schemes. This quiet piano music, Chopin I think it was, laying down a strange soundtrack as I droove past neds at the beginning of their drinking career. They're that gullible at the height of their arrogance, they don't see what's coming even though it's all around if they care to look. The pianist's hand came down soft like a branch in the breeze, sounding the soft notes and finding a well of emotions deep in. Like he was searching specifically and selecting guilt. Guilt at how Danny could have slipped so far so quick. And Billy too for that matter. And Shelly.

There was nothing I could do. Yesterday's history, tomorrow's a mystery. I stopped and was about to phone my sponsor. But I clicked off and instead phoned my son, Joe. Asked if he fancied a movie, a pizza, a burger; something normal. Thank fuck he agreed.

# Summer 1998

I came home that scorching evening to tap my Da
money and found Danny curled up on a wooden
chair. He was crying and when he lifted his head
he was some mess. His eyes were puffed up and
his bottom lip was bust so that blood and saliva ran
onto his chin and dripped onto the floor. His nose
was broke.

—What the fuck happened to you? I said, putting
my wine down.

He mumbled something and I wet an old cloth.
I wiped his face from the brow first, slow and
methodical, checking for cuts as I went. When I
wrapped my hand round the back of his head I could
feel lumps coming up. He winced when I got to his
nose and I gave him the cloth for his lips. As he
dabbed away you could see his pain. I poured what
was left of the Buckie into two old china cups.

—What happened?

He burst out loud this time and I waited till he'd
bubbled some wine down.

—Danny, who the fuck done this to you?

—Billy Brown, he said.

I jumped up and punched the door.

—I warned that cunt the last time.

—Leave it Stevie, Danny said.

—Where is he?

—Leave it.

—Where the fuck is he Danny?

—I gave him cheek. I deserved it.

—What? Ye gave him cheek? Ye deserve this for a bit of cheek?

—It was my fault, I don't want nothing done about it.

He went to the sink and started washing his face. I knew anger wasn't the way to go so, even though my heart was a horse, I tried to be calm.

—D'ye think ye need stitches?

He nodded no.

It was just me and him and the running water. When the tap went off the room was filled with the sound of gentle lather and crackle of him soaping his face.

—Here, let me do that.

I sat him in a chair and leaned him back, soaped his face in small slow circles like a baby. I filled a basin with clean water and spent half an hour cleaning his face. In this heat it was soothing slipping my hands into that cold water. He wasn't so bad when I removed the dried blood. A bad cut to the lip but the rest was scuffs and bruises, but still, when he went to look in the lobby mirror, he burst out crying. He came back in and said he was going to his bed.

—Where's my Da? I said.

He shrugged.

—Was going to tap him to go back down the pub. Got any spare?

He held a tenner out but didn't actually give it to me. Instead he stared a question.

—I won't, I said.

—Promise, he said.

—I promise.

—On my Maw's grave.

—Aw come on to fuck!

—On my Maw's grave, Stevie.

—I promise on my Maw's grave.

—What?

—That I won't go looking for Billy Brown.

—No – say it all in the one sentence.

—I promise on my mother's grave that I won't go looking for Billy Brown.

He gave me the tenner and I could see tears coming before he turned and walked away.

I was having a good time in Dempsey's and worked my way into some pretty company. Gave them the crack. They were going to Targets and the one with the Spanish hair and the green eyes asked if I was going. Too right I was. I bounced up to get the last round.

And something happened. Something happened like something often happens on the drink; a switch flicks or a light goes off, or on, or a shutter comes down or lifts. Something.

Happens.

When I put the drinks down I was dark and they

noticed. The buzz dropped from that table and they started fixing their jackets and bags. Drinking up, and by the time they'd left I was staring into my pint. I sat straight up and breathed deep and deliberate through my nose, downed my pint and headed off.

Guys were going about in shorts with their shirts in their hands. The sweat was running down my back and it was three in the morning by the time I found out where he was.

I crossed the park keeping my eyes at the window. There was a few of them moving about. Looked like they were dancing. And colours. Yellow. White. But mainly red. I didn't know if the red was coming from the window or my anger.

The close smelt of hot sticky piss. I banged on the door and a lassie about fifteen answered, the sweat was running down her tanned skin.

—Billy there?

She laughed and said she'd go and get him.

I was wound up to lay into the bastard when Santa Claus appeared.

—Ho ho ho, he said.

—Who the fuck're you?

—Mister Claus. AKA Santa, or Santy to you my man.

But it was Billy Brown's voice behind the beard and when he asked did I want to sit on his knee I stuck the head on him.

They were all screaming when I threw that bastard against the railings and laid into his fluffy beard with hard rights. He wailed and scrabbled away. But I got him by the legs and dragged him back.

—What've I done? What've I done?

—Shut fuckin up, I said and kicked him in the red ribs. Somebody came to another door and in that distraction he made for the stairs but I swung out on the railings and caught him an almighty kick in the back. He tumbled beard over tit to the bottom and lay there groaning. I went down and lifted him by the hat.

—Touch my brother again and I'll fuckin kill ye.

There was a look in his eyes.

—He never touched Danny, came this voice from up the close.

—What?

—It was your Da that done it. Him and Danny were fighting. Over the park this afternoon. Your Da got lifted.

I looked at Santa lying on the floor, his beard red with blood, and outside the birds already whistling.

# 2008

Shelly ended up with pancreatitis with the booze out the community centre. It was serious touch and go stuff. Danny and Billy wouldn't leave her bedside. My Maw was praying Shelly would die and the shock would send Danny back to AA. With me just started seeing Penelope I felt Danny and me were accelerating away from each other.

Things were getting worse all round for him. I don't know if it was my Maw's prayers backfiring or just missing the mark but, one day at visiting, Billy went into an alcoholic seizure and they banged him in ward twenty-four and filled him with diazepam.

So Danny was on his own and kept himself topped up, scared in case he went the way Billy went. A week passed and Shelly wasn't getting any better. I went in twice after I'd dropped Penelope off at her work but Danny didn't really want to see me. He had a head full of AA and a belly full of drink. Everything we'd built as brothers in AA had been wiped away. I decided not to visit any more. Told him if he seen me in the hospital not to take a resentment cos we both know the score. He hung his head and said aye. I told him I loved him and left.

My Maw went up every other day but more to see Danny than Shelly. Not unless she was casting secret spells on her. She'd come home and tell us Danny was sober, looking great, shining like a new pin, but I knew better. He was keeping himself at a level he could cope with; his need for drink battling his need for Shelly. But if she was in there long enough the drink would win. Booze always wins in the end. It's cunning, baffling and powerful.

Another week passed and Danny got all the books, his, Billy's and Shelly's and cashed them. It was hundreds of pounds. The government was paying them to drink. Danny came out the post office with the buzz of anticipation in his solar plexus. In Haddows, as he eyed the rows of beautiful bottles, he could taste alcohol on the back of his tongue.

He never made the hospital that day and Shelly missed him. Through the morphine clouds she could always see Danny arriving like an angel, hear his wings as he landed and feel the voluptuousness of his lips as he kissed hers; cracked and dry. But this day the clouds kept passing and no angel Danny, no beating wings. Sometimes a bird would go by and she'd strain as if to lift then fall back and it would be gone.

Danny woke up impregnated with guilt and surrounded by booze. He sat cross-legged on the floor, chin on his chest, sobbing. Set about drinking but swore he'd never miss the hospital again. Poor Shelly. Poor Shelly, he said out loud to himself all the way up, even in the lift. Shelly managed to squeeze out a few words.

—Where were ye baby? Yesterday?

—Couldn't face seeing you like this, he said, —I just got drunk.

Shelly squeezed his hand. She understood. It was nothing to do with her being like that. It was drink. That's the way it worked.

It was the next day my Maw heard the story. Danny had a bottle of vodka and was giving Shelly sips now and then. They asked him to take it outside or hand it over so he went out and drank it in three goes.

Now he's out his head meandering back to Shelly. Now he's in the lift pressing what he thinks is six. The lift went down.

Now he's in the labyrinth. Corridors, doorways, portals, wires and ducts going every way and him doubling and trebling everything. When he took a step forwards he had three feet. He started following numbers on the ducting thinking he was heading for wards but every ward was a metal door that wouldn't open. Danny was kicking dents in one when he heard shouting.

—Right you, stop right there!

A silhouette at the thin end of a mathematical corridor sounded like it was running but looked like it was standing still. Danny bolted. And that's the thing with alkies when they're pished, there's no logic to them. They swerve and turn to puzzling impulses. Danny was in the heart of the labyrinth in minutes. He could hear muffled echoes as he sat on a hot pipe. He doesn't know if he fell asleep but next thing he remembers is the silence down there except for the whirring and clicking of machines, the odd beep now and then and this nauseating sense that Shelly was plugged into all this, that the wires and nozzles coming out of her body connected into this abomination. He ran shouting her name.

—Shelly! Shelly!! Shelly!!!

Then, up ahead, a slither of white clinical light. Chill hit him when he opened that door.

—Shelly!

She was lying naked under a white sheet. He knew it was her before he pulled the sheet off and there she was. But now, in death, as beautiful as Billy swore she once was, like the photos at fifteen when Billy met her. She was white as communion. Danny let out a low moan, knelt down and held onto her. Her body was cold and stiff.

—Oh Shelly, Shelly. What am I going to do? What am I going to do?

He kissed her hand over and over and didn't turn when he heard the footsteps. The security guy comforted Danny and sent his mate for the chaplin.

It was the same priest that had officiated at Liam Brown's funeral. Danny recognised him, through the booze and the grief.

—Father, Father, she's…

—That's okay my son, he said, —that's okay.

He held Danny and gave security the nod. They stood in the corridor. They were solemn and silent.

Father Dover got on his knees.

—Let us pray.

He started a rosary and Danny mumbled a few words here and there. By now he had his back to the trolley and his legs straight out, muttering Shelly's name over and over.

—Shelly! Oh Shelly. Shelly…

When the rosary was finished the priest coaxed Danny away and took him to the cafeteria, filled him with black coffee and got the whole story out of him. That's when he realised who Danny was.

—Are you Annie's son? he said.

—Aye Father.

—Ah, I thought I recognised you. Asda!

—Mm mm Father.

—You and Billy is it?

Danny nodded.

—Oh and that girl, what's her name now?

—Shelly, Father, said Danny and rolled into tears again.

A queer look came over Father Dover. He said he'd be back in a minute and headed back to the morgue.

Danny decided to let Billy know the bad news. Billy let out a wail that shook the hospital to its foundations. The rest of the nutters and junkies and alkies in ward twenty-four slunk under their sheets in case whatever it was, was coming for them.

—I have to go up and get her belongings Danny, Billy said.

But they wouldn't let Billy out the ward.

—My wife's dead! Billy was shouting as Danny left but they'd heard it all on twenty-four.

When Danny arrived the priest was standing beside Shelly's bed chatting away. Danny gawped at Shelly, gawped at the priest.

—What have ye done Father?

The priest tried to speak but Danny dove on Shelly, kissing every inch of her face.

—Oh thank you Father, thank you, thank you, thank you. It's a miracle. Send for Billy! Tell him she's came alive again!

Danny knelt and kissed Father Dover's hand.

—Thanks Father. I'll never miss the chapel again.

The priest didn't know to laugh or boot Danny up the arse but he knew my Maw and as soon as he could free his hand he headed down to tell her the whole story. Him and my Da sat drinking and laughing but my Maw, all she could think about was that poor lonely lassie in the morgue.

Billy snuck out twenty-four and when he seen Shelly alive he attacked Danny. The fight spilled into the corridor and all the heart monitors' frequencies went up. They got lifted and released next morning without charge; all the argument gone out of them.

Shelly got out a week after that. My Maw met them outside Asda dancing and celebrating. A massive cargo they had.

—Should you be drinking hen, with you just out the hospital and that?

—They told me it was okay Annie.

—Are ye sure?

—Aye. They said as long as I lay off it a couple of days now and then, that right Billy?

Billy nodded it was indeed right and my Maw shook her head and walked away.

But Penelope found out the exact situation. If Shelly drank again she'd die.

# Winter 1998

On the site on the Monday Liam Brown wanted to know if we got our money.

—Aye we fuckin did, I said.

But he didn't believe us. We had a bit of an argument about spilling concrete over the pans. It was a stand-off but with no vibes of violence and my thinking was, even though he didn't say it, Liam would make sure his squad was careful next pour.

We were downing six tins of Super a day each, enough to stay topped-up but still work. And we were that happy getting the money and keeping our jobs we played a few jokes. It was Danny's idea.

On the Tuesday it was minus ten and everything was welded thegether with frost. All the men were in the hut with condensation streaming down the windows and when we eventually got the courage to go out into that cold morning it was all creaking oilskins and blowing into gloves. Same again at the ten o clock break. Danny and me tanned another can each to my Da's tutting disgust.

—That's how your uncle Paul got bumped off the sites, he said.

But we didn't care. He never drank at work, my

Da, although he made up for it at nights. Danny posted his can out the window. I crushed mine and spun it through the door onto the canal where it skated the ice and crashed into the reeds.

An amazing thing happened when we came out. The can Danny posted out the window was standing upright, to attention. And another thing: it was perfect kicking distance from the hut door. What I mean by that is; when you came out and took one step it put you exactly in position to boot that can into orbit. Like you'd do with rugby ball. I went to give it a hefty boot but Danny pulled me back.

—No.

He lifted the can and marked an X in the frost with the heel of his boot.

—What the fuck're yees up to now? my Da said and walked past shaking his head.

Danny got a three feet metal spike and a giant sledgehammer. We took turns at hammering that spike into the hard ground till only four inches poked up. A mole's periscope. Danny punched a hole in the bottom of the can and hid it under the hut. Then we went to work.

At dinner time the hut was thronged with men eating farting and talking shite. We gave Billy a can of Super on the fly. Now and then he'd drink with us on the quiet. Brother or not Liam would've sacked him. When everybody was eating Danny went outside, got the can and placed it over the spike.

Me and Danny sat at the window watching men leave in ones and twos. They just walked round the thing. None of them was tempted. Danny had long lanky legs. Maybe we hammered the spike too far away? Liam and Billy left. Billy thought about it but walked on. Liam walked past too and the trick was lost. But Liam turned back and lined himself to kick it onto the canal.

—Watch this Billy, he said, —right over the other end.

He swivelled his hips and penalty-kicked that can. Well. The can gave a slight wobble and the shock thrummed up Liam's leg, detonating at the knee, rippling up the thigh, exploding at the hip. Down he went, a delicious scream screeching out as he deflated, his face turning up to heaven. Billy lifted the can revealing the spike. Then the two of them spotted me and Danny howling down silently, wiping the condensation for a better look.

When we got out Liam had his welly, carrier bag and sock off, rubbing his toes with a grimace. They weren't even steel-toed his wellies and that made us laugh all the more.

—Ya pair of cunts, said Billy. But there was a smile on his face too.

On the Wednesday Danny had decided to come off the drink. He brung a big plastic bottle of Irn-Bru and was slugging as we got our gear on. Liam was limping. When we came in for the morning break

somebody had been slugging at Danny's Irn-Bru.
It was quarter down.

—Right who's been drinking this? he said and held
it above his head. Nobody admitted up and he sat
down. Was probably more than one of them that
drank it. You come in the hut, you see a big bottle of
Irn-Bru, you have a spy out the window, nocunt
watching; you take a slug.

At dinner time the same, another quarter gone.
Danny holds the bottle up.

—Right ya bunch of cunts, he says. —Who's been
drinking this?

No answer.

The pour that afternoon went well. Concrete in
the shutters and any that fell outside of the pans,
Liam and Billy washed off with buckets of water;
the hoses being all froze up. We had to work late
cos the concrete kept coming till the section was
poured. We covered it up to keep it warm and
the gaffer gave us an afternoon break between
jaegers.

First thing was Danny holding up the Irn-Bru.

—Right. Who the fuck's been at this again?

No takers. Danny pointed to the label. There was
something wrote in pencil.

—See that, he said and drew his finger along the
line. —Can none of yees fuckin read?

He had their attention now. Danny read it like
they were primary kids.

—Do – not – drink – this – cos – I – have – pished – in – it!

There was silence and then Liam spoke.

—What time at? he asked.

The hut burst out laughing. Liam washed his mouth out with cold tea and spat it all over Danny but Danny kept right on laughing. Everybody was laughing and repeating Liam's *what time at* line. And we were still laughing when the next jaeger came. We burst onto the site, the story of Liam and the Irn-Bru booming round the place. There was a half jaeger of concrete left at the end and the gaffer asked Liam's men to make a path to the huts with it. He'd pay them. Liam agreed but you could see he wasn't happy. We checked the bolt alignment and fucked off.

—See ye later Liam, have a nice night ya pish guzzler.

On Thursday Liam and Billy were there when we arrived.

—Nice path, said Danny.

—Been here all night? I said and laughed.

I slipped out of my boots and tried to shove my foot into my welly and stumbled over. Danny was the same. Billy and Liam were laughing and I thought it was my stumble until I tried to pick my welly up. Considering a foot square of concrete weighs a hundredweight you can imagine how heavy that welly was. Filled to the rim and set solid. Both of them. And Danny's. And the pockets of our oilskins.

—Heavee man, Liam said. —Heavee!

Me and Danny went about that site like two rookies: brand-new oilskins and brand-new wellies. That was it. They'd got their own back. We made a truce.

At dinner time on Friday the gaffer handed out the cheques. We half-expected Sterling to have deducted the money for the busted pans but my Da said it was all A-okay. Hip to the groove. Not a curdy deducted.

But Liam and Billy came bursting into the hut fighting like fuck. There was something wrong with their cheque. Liam sat down with a pen working something out while Billy gripped the edge of the table. All his fingers were white with rage. Nobody said nothing.

—Much? Billy said.

—Five hundred and seventy-five, said Liam and underlined it three times with a red ballpoint, scoring right through to the table.

I nodded to my Da and Danny to get out of there. We went on site and continued striking yesterday's pans. Laying them out for the next section of the ring beam. That was to be our last day.

Liam and Billy came tumbling out and stormed across that site, their boots crashing through iced up pot-holes. We watched them arguing with the gaffer who shrugged, looked at the numbers and shook his

head. Liam shouted some more then I seen the gaffer
point over at us. Liam made the connection and
started in a sprint towards us.

He went chest to chest with me.

—What's your fuckin game?

—What the fuck're ye on about?

He slapped the paper repeatedly into my face.

—This, he kept saying, —the pans. The fuckin
concrete.

—Do that one more time and I'll kick your cunt in
Liam.

Bang!

He caught me a right hook that sent me reeling
sideways. I swung a boot catching him under the ribs.
He doubled up and I managed to get a few in before
Billy set about me. Danny dragged Billy off and they
were rolling about in the frost. The rest of the men
had run over to watch. Cheering and shouting. Liam
had regained enough sense to lay some methodicals
into me. Ribs, ribs, head, hook, jab. It was blue flash
after blue flash. I got hold of the cunt just as the
gaffer came ripping through the crowd. I had a
knack for these short hefty hooks that men with
strong chests and shoulder can fling. Liam *oofed* a
few times. Close up his technical punches were like
lassies' cos he needed distance to damage. And by
fuck was I making sure he couldn't get it. Every time
he tried to step back I grabbed his shirt, pulled him
in, bear-hugged him, let go and fired a couple of

hooks in. I was glad to see the gaffer's face between me and him. He wedged in and shoved us apart. By now people going to B and Q were stopping. Billy and Danny had been separated. Both looked equally battered.

That's when I seen Sterling's car. It was empty but I knew he was somewhere watching. That was his plan: turn us against each other, get us to do his dirty work; to each other.

Then, Liam started arguing with the gaffer. It started sensible but then they both took a step back into fighting positions. I'd never thought of the gaffer as a fighter but now he looked big and capable. Although the men were shouting *don't be daft Liam* and all that, you could feel they wanted this fight to go ahead out of curiosity. The gaffer let go with a good uppercut. But Liam instinctively leaned and it only clipped him and continued upwards. When the gaffer's arm was still in the air Liam laid six in. Broke his nose. Two cracked ribs. The gaffer fell to the ground and rolled in a ball but Liam still laid in. This was vicious. Liam took a lot out on him.

That was us all sacked and black-listed. None of us ever worked on the sites again. Sterling got the cops. And there was enough guys on that site wanting to keep their jobs for a truth to come out. They lifted Liam out Dempsey's a week after that. He pleaded guilty and got a year. Every letter he sent to Billy had a section on what he was going to do to me on his release date. As for the rest of us, me, Danny, Billy and my Da. We drank that wee bit more. The booze held our hands and led us on.

# 2009

Danny had been in hospital three days when we found out. My Maw phoned me; he'd been stabbed eighty times. The old rage came back and a deep, deep instinct for revenge but by the time I reached the hospital sense had kicked in.

Until I seen Danny that is.

He was on all sorts of crazy machines with dials and bleepers. Wires were growing out of his body, tubes going in and pipes coming out. Shelly was crying at the bedside. She had a pair of rosary beads and she was mumbling. My Maw was at the other side clapping Danny. I say clapping cos she was running her hand down his hair like a puppy. She wasn't crying now my Maw. My shoulder twitched to punch something, the door maybe. But I controlled and hugged my Maw. She said my Da was on the rampage looking for the guys that done it. He was on the drink fulla madness. She hoped he'd kill the three of them. Slow. They lived in the high flats, she said, and told me the floor and the door number. You didn't need to be a psychologist to see what she wanted me to do. She was revenge. I was the weapon. I said nothing and sat down. My Maw joined in with Shelly's prayers. The nurse told me she'd been sleeping on the floor in Danny's room.

—There's love for you, she said. —You could learn things from them.

I spent two hours trying to get what happened but Shelly stuttered and garbled it. My Maw kept butting in with anger, mixing Shelly up. I asked Shelly if she wanted to go for a curry. She didn't want to leave Danny but I convinced her an hour away and maybe a couple of drinks would do her a world of good.

Once I got her fed I bought her a strong lager. She hadn't drank for days and guzzled it in two. I knew what would happen next. She needed another drink. I asked her to tell me what happened but she shook her head. She was too terrified to talk. The guys were going to kill Danny if she told anybody anything and she heard a rumour they were going to come and get me too. She watched me rebound from that then nodded to the bar.

—Goanny get us another lager? she said.

I ordered it and biting back the fear, when the waiter put the glass down, I put my hand over it.

—Shelly, I said, —I need to know what happened. Especially if they're threatening me an all now.

I could see she regretted telling me that. The story she came away with, as I kept her alcohol level steady was this: it was a Monday, the three of them cash their books every second good Monday. By midnight they were pished and were heading home. They went through the new cycle path as a shortcut.

Halfway down three neds were sat drinking. Shelly says Danny asked for a slug of their lager. They told him to fuck off and an argument started. Danny couldn't beat Casey's drum but he had a mouth like Muhammad Ali and he starts giving the neds abuse. This guy, he was only fifteen Shelly says, he pulls a blade and goes for Danny. Got him on the ground slashing and stabbing like a madman. The other two sat on the wall drinking and laughing, she said. Drinking and laughing.

—D'ye want a drink? the fifteen-year-old was saying. —D'ye want a drink? Here's a fuckin drink. Drink blood ya jakie bastard.

Danny's arms were flailing about and he was screaming. There was blood everywhere. The two on the wall started chanting. Like a football song, she said.

—Kill the jakie! Kill the jakie give us peace. Kill the jakie give us peace!

He kept stabbing till Danny stopped moving. Shelly dove in and lay on Danny so he had to stab her to get to him. And he did. He stabbed her twice on the leg to get her off.

—D'you want to see the stitches? she asked, and started unbuttoning her jeans.

—No. It's alright. What happened next?

The fifteen-year-old screamed at her to get off so he could plunge Danny but she wouldn't move. She wrapped herself round him…

Shelly stopped. I thought she was pausing. Or

maybe it was too horrific. But she finished the latest lager and asked for another one.

—What happened next Shelly?

—Next?

—Aye. How did you get away?

She said they left. I wanted to know how that came about. Did the cops come? Or did her and Danny run? Or did the other two neds stop it? But she was blank. She didn't remember. Then I thought; wait a minute – what was Billy doing all this time?

—Where was Billy? I said.

She looked at me. —Billy?

—Aye, did Billy not do something?

She shook her head. —Billy ran away.

Now I knew Billy from long ago. Since Danny was a baby. I fuckin drank with Billy. He had the heart of a lion and even taking in the fear that gathers with age and the frailty of the alky, I couldn't believe Billy would run. Billy was a boxer, Billy was a fuckin street fighting machine. I had three tangles with Billy when we were young and he beat me all three. Beat me good an all. I couldn't see him running. I could see him lifting a stick and challenging, I could see him throwing rocks to get them off Danny, I could see him getting them to chase him. But not running. Not Billy. He might be a lot of things, Billy, but he's no coward. Billy Brown came with a guarantee.

—I don't believe Billy ran away, Shelly.

—He did. And I shouted not to show his face near my house again.

—I still can't believe he ran away.

Shelly assured me soon as the knife came out Billy ran. But Billy was a noted blade man himself. If you beat him in a square go you better watch out. Cos one dark night Billy would appear like the devil and slash slash stab, down you'd go with his voice ringing in your ears.

—No cunt beats Billy Brown.

I looked her straight in the eye.

—Why did Billy not pull his blade out Shelly?

She was angry now.

—I don't know – he ran. Billy ran.

—Then what happened?

—I don't know. I can't remember.

She was drawing attention to us. So I ordered another lager and an orange juice and asked what exactly she did remember.

She remembered being on the ground. Next thing they were running, her and Danny, the three guys shouting they were going to kill him. But he kept running and she kept up. An ice cream van stopped. The woman thought Danny had been in a car accident, there was so much blood. They gave him a fag and he sat on the kerb smoking and chatting with drunk bravado. He didn't realise how bad it was. An ambulance came and by the hospital Danny was unconscious.

—What did you not contact us for Shelly, that night?

—I love him. I only wanted to be beside him. I never thought.

She drank back the lager and she was crying.
Her tears ran round the glass and down her chin.

—I have to get back up to see Danny. Can you buy
me some flowers? I always buy him flowers.

I bought flowers at the garage and let her go
in herself. I couldn't face Danny again. I droove up
the canal and sat looking at the stars in the water.
Wave after wave of hatred for these cunts droove
through me. This was a night that could change my
life forever. I could be back in the jail without hope
if I couldn't control myself. I forced my mind to see
clearly. Think think think. Twice I started the engine
and droove towards my Maw's to get that exact
address. Twice I droove back. I was sick with fear
and the metallic taste of adrenaline. My mouth
was dry and the swans drifted over the canal. Think
think think. At least I didn't have a weapon. Think
think think. What would somebody sensible do?
The old gods were screaming *kill kill kill.* But these
other more serene gods, they were saying, *take it
through the channels. Take it through the right
channels.* But what were they? The right channels?
Think think think. The cops, of course. That's what it
was. The cops.

I slept in the car listening to these nuns chanting
'A Mass For The End of Time'. Had it on repeat.
In the morning I took six rolls and six square slice
sausages to my Maw's. I was going to get the address
and give it to the cops. My Maw was up but my Da
was in bed with a hangover. He'd been in the flats

all night drinking and waiting but either they'd not turned up or they'd seen him. Even after three rolls an sausage my Maw still wanted revenge but I managed to persuade her to go to the cops. Take it through the right channels. Cos there's no telling what these wee cunts'll do next. It was only when I even hinted I would see them after they got the jail that she cheered up and off we went up the cop station.

But Danny had to make the complaint himself this cop said.

—What, he's lying up there hanging onto life and he's got to make a complaint himself?

The cop shrugged and I ranted on.

—If it was some rich cunt that got stabbed eighty times you'd not be waiting on them making a complaint would you?

He said he knew how we felt and I said, —Aye discriminated against for being white fuckin trash. Get out there and arrest them – there's their addresses.

My Maw handed over a bit of paper. He sighed, went away and came back with another cop. CID. He said he was going up the hospital to see Shelly. Get a statement. Take it from there.

I took my Maw home. Had a coffee with my Da convincing him not to take revenge. When I left I was sure it was all going through the right channels. There was two witnesses. Billy before he ran away and Shelly who remembered every Technicolor detail. These wee cunts were getting banged up for a long time. If Shelly wasn't making it up. You never know with alkies. They'll say anything. Lie even when they don't need to. They're scared of truth.

Two days later I came in from walking along the canal thinking about nothing but the sky and the different grades of colour and texture on the water. There was a message from my Maw. Could I phone?

I got my Da. He was raging again. I thought he'd been drinking but I wasn't sure. Shelly's telling the CID she can't remember a thing. Danny's still unconscious, Billy Brown's nowhere to be seen and the cops say there's nothing they can do. My Da was going out tonight to get them. And he had called some people to get a wee message. He hung up.

I knew he wanted me to go with him. He was taunting me. In the middle of that dark and muddled world there was a big electromagnet pulling me in. It didn't matter how far into space I floated, I was always in orbit of the same planet. One day its gravity would get me.

Two hours later I was standing right where Danny got stabbed. I looked up and down that path. It was the sort of place you could lie dead for days. A perfect spot for a mugger except that people never came that way because it was a perfect spot for muggers. I scanned. Somebody tried to kill my brother here. You'd think you'd feel some vibes but there was nothing. It was all about time and change. Same spot; different time. There was a fifteen-foot fence that reminded me of jail. And behind it rows and rows of cars. And then I seen it; high on a pole, watching these cars, a CCTV camera.

The guy in the garage was wary but when I told him I was looking for evidence to pass onto the cops he let me into the tea room where the tapes were.

—What night was it?

—Last Monday. About midnight.

He gets a tape, shoves it in and puts it on fast-forward. There was nothing on that path. Nothing at all. Only supersonic fast-forward birds passing made you realise it wasn't a photo. Then, in the distance, walking like Charlie Chaplin – three figures. *That'll be the three neds* I thought, but it wasn't. I pressed play and the tape slowed to Danny, Shelly and Billy Brown. Arguing. The way jakies always argue. Pointing and shouting. Even though there was no sound I could hear their shouts. But where were the three guys? The three neds? Where were...

—Fuck!

The tape went blank.

—Sometimes that happens, the guy said. —It runs out and we don't change it till the next shift.

I thanked him and droove off. When I told my Da about the tape he said the three guys must've been hiding. He wouldn't listen when I said there was nobody else there. That it was Billy Brown that stabbed Danny. But my Da's revenge was set on three non-existent neds. And he didn't want to re-direct it. Two pals were coming tonight and they were bringing that wee message.

—A message? Are you mad? You could end up doing life for the wrong guys.

When my Maw came in she was sure it wasn't Billy. Sure, had Danny not gave Billy a hell of a doing a fortnight earlier? Billy would be scared of Danny, he's like a pile of sticks now Billy Brown, he'd break if you kissed him too hard.

—Danny battered Billy?

—Aye, last week, she said.

—Well then! I said.

—Well then what?

But proof of one thing to my Maw and Da was proof of another to me.

—Try this version of the story out for size, I said. —Danny moves in with Billy Brown and his wife Shelly. Eventually Shelly fancies Danny and ousts Billy so Danny's Shelly's man now but Billy, the ex-husband, still lives in the same house. Tell me there's no ill feeling there.

But my Maw says they're happy with that arrangement.

—So, I tells her, —there's an underlying resentment to say the least. Two weeks before the stabbing Danny gives Billy a right doing. Billy was in Casualty. Kept in overnight. Danny batters Billy in front of his ex-wife. Billy wants revenge. When's the best time to take that revenge? When Danny's too drunk to stand.

—You're havering, my Da says.

—There was only three people on that path, I said,

—three people. Danny, Shelly and Billy. Danny's drunk. Billy's been drinking all day too but keeping himself kinda sober and they're staggering home at midnight. They get to where they can't be seen by anybody and Billy stabs Danny. Sets about him before he can defend himself. Slashes and stabs. Shelly jumps on Danny to save him. Billy's got a rep for blades and this kind of revenge. And I dare say the revenge he took out on Danny wasn't only the revenge for the doing. Billy sees how far he's gone and runs. Shelly gets Danny to the main road then the hospital. There's no way she's sticking Billy in. That's her ex-husband. So she makes up a story about three neds. And when Danny comes round he doesn't want to stick Billy in either so he goes along with Shelly's story.

My Maw and Da thought it was too far-fetched.

—Okay, I said. —What do you do if you're out with your mates one night and a serious fight starts and your bottle crashes and you run away. What do you do?

They didn't know so I told them.

—You turn up next day riddled with guilt and remorse. You turn up looking for forgiveness. You make up an excuse. You say you were fighting with two of them and it was too much. Or the cops came. Or you got knocked out and when you woke up there was nobody there. You don't stay away. That's the last thing you do; stay away. You need to know what happened. Is your mate alright? You only stay away if you attacked your mate. Attacked him so bad he might die. You go into fuckin hiding. And where's Billy Brown? Nobody's seen him for a week. And why did Shelly shout Billy better not come near her door again? She shouted that cos Billy had just stabbed Danny to bits and ran.

After that was silence.

# 2009

When me and my Maw and Da walked in Shelly shoved the cider bottle under the sheets. Danny was asleep and as he breathed in and out I swear I could hear the blood on the stitches cracking. The state he was in it was hard to believe he was alive.

—Billy done it didn't he? I said.

Shelly was a rabbit caught in headlights.

—Was it Billy Brown that bliddy done that to Danny? said my Maw.

She shook her head.

—Tell me where he is, my Da said with finality.

—It wasn't Billy, said Shelly.

But everybody in that room knew it was Billy.

—What did you tell him not to come back near your door for, Shelly? I said.

—Cos he ran away.

—Aye – after he done that to Danny.

My Maw burst out crying and got down beside Danny.

—How's he not came up the hospital to see Danny? my Maw asked.

—He ran away, is all Shelly could say, —Billy ran away.

My Da got hold of her.

—Where is he?

—Fuckin leave me alone! she shouted, —Nurse! Nurse! The nurse came in. My Maw tried one last time.

—Just tell us it was Billy, Shelly, she said.

—I don't want to talk about it any more. And she reached under the sheets, took out the cider and drank it at us. Her two eyes filled with loathing, white and bulbous over the curve of the bottle.

# 1995

My Maw and Da were trying the *buy him everything, treat him great* approach. Trying to get through to him but I knew it was too late with Danny. They bought him a two hundred pound leather jacket, a hundred quid pair of Nike trainers and a hundred and fifty quid boogie box. Pump up the volume. It wasn't his birthday or anything. They bought him all that stuff out the blue. After they gave him it my Da said, —Look Danny see when ye go out the night, why don't ye try just having a few drinks?

—Come home, have a wee chat and go to bed, my Maw says. —Like a civilised son.

—Try it anyway? asked my Da.

Danny agreed to try and swaggered out with that boogie box on his shoulder. Crushing the whole scheme with sound waves. Bobbing up and down. He reverberated into the idiotic distance. But give him his due, Danny, he came home pretty sober that night. By usual standards.

♫ Where did you come from where did you go where did you come from Cotton Eyed Joe?

But night by night he got steadily drunker till he was as bad as ever, lying on the grass outside Dempsey's with the batteries draining till even the music sounded drunk. He was attracting attention with all that expensive gear and his big mouth. He was embarrassing and I'm not ashamed to say I avoided him. Round about that time Liam Brown met me in Dempsey's.

—You better got a hold of your Danny, Liam said. —He's out there assaulting everybody.

—Our Danny? Fuckin Chicken George? Assaulting who?

—Everycunt, Liam says. —He's assaulting everycunt.

—What with? A baseball bat?

—No, says Liam. —Your name!

I had a few beers with Liam. He'd had the same trouble with Billy but he sorted that out by putting Billy into the boxing. Billy turned out to be a great boxer.

—I'm giving you the early warning here Stevie, said Liam. —Cos it'll cause ye no end of fucking trouble.

I went out and slapped Danny about a wee bit. Told him he better fight his own battles. If he's big enough to mouth off he's big enough to take the consequences but he kept slabbering and trying to hug me.

—We're brothers, he kept saying, — brothers, and brothers are like that, he said and locked his hands thegether like some demented prayer. He played 'La Bamba' at me as I walked away.

My wife had not long flung me out then and I was staying short term in my Maw's. That night I heard Danny and my Da arguing. A fight broke out and the next day both of them were marked. I decided to get out of there. I took a flat off the blitz list and moved in the same day.

Next week my Da arrived in some mood. Danny had came in covered in sick minus his jacket and boogie box, he'd tried to get some sense out of him but he was rubber out his head. Next morning my Da got up at the crack of dawn and caught Danny trying to escape at six. That's the thing with alkies, they're up with the birds craving that first drink of the day. Outside the packie's waiting for it to open, chatting and rubbing their hands thegether.

So my Da questioned him.

—I can't remember, Danny was saying.

—You must remember something.

—I can't fuckin remember, goanny let me out?

But my Da barred the way. Danny sat on the stairs crying. He remembered lying on the grass. Then a few guys dragging him around by the boogie box. He eventually had to let go. They kicked and wrestled him out of his jacket.

—Who were they?

—I'm not a grass, said Danny.

—A grass? A fuckin grass! screamed my Da. —They fuckin mugged ye!

—I'm not grassing, said Danny.

—I want a name.

But Danny sat saying nothing, tears running down his cheeks. Then my Da had a bright idea. He pulled out a twenty.

—A name, he said.

Danny looked at the money. Looked at the clock. It was nearly seven.

—Techno, he said.

—Techno? What kind of a fuckin name is that?

—That's his name. Techno.

—What does he look like, this Techno?

—Red hair. Dances like this.

And David waved his hands above his head like a mental inmate.

—I don't give two fucks what he dances like, where does he live?

My Da gave Danny the twenty, but blocked his way still.

—Brewer Street, said Danny.

My Da let him go.

Brewer Street was a noted no-go area. My Da thought about getting the cops but what good would they do? They wouldn't even get out their car. It was hard to tell if they had legs these days, the cops. So what did he want to do? He wanted me and him to get this cunt Techno. It was seven at night and I'd had a few tins and a bottle of Buckie but no joints. Drink was like aeroplane fuel with me if I didn't temper it with the dope.

—Right, I said. —Let's go.

My Da wasn't ready for that kind of decisiveness.

—Should we not plan it a wee bit first?

—Plan? I said. —Here's the plan. Go down to Brewer Street, get the cunt, get the stuff back.

Out we went.

Brewer Street was on a steep hill. My Da turned into the bottom. He had an old Chrysler at the time. I could see a bunch at the top partying. Moving their hands in the air like Danny said.

We switched the lights off and droove up the hill in the dark. Passed them. I spotted somebody with red hair. When we went back I seen him again. Red hair, freckles, biggest mouth. They glared in the car this time and some walked towards us, getting faster as we sped away. Shouting. I knew next time would be bricks and bottles.

—Drive back up, I said.

—Back up?

—Aye. Stop right beside them.

My Da's face was a picture as we droove up. Some stood on the road to stop us. My Da slowed but I put my leg over and pressed the accelerator. They scattered. I shouted stop and pulled the handbrake on, the car screeched to a halt and I sprang out, leaving the door wide.

—What one of yous is called Techno? I said.

Techno was on the wall as gallous as you like. To tell you the truth I was surprised at his confidence.

—I'm Techno – how?

Bang! I broke his nose. The back of his head was against the fence and I felt the thudding impact. Instinctively he put his hands to his face. The rest of the neds were in shock-pause. By this time my Da was standing beside me. I leaned into Techno.

—I want the stuff back.

I turned to go to the car. Three neds were in my road. But they were already wavering. I stared and they moved.

My Da started the engine. I wound the window down and glared as we droove away. Nobody moved. When we turned the corner at the bottom the two of us cheered.

We got a carry-out and celebrated. I was electric all night. The rush of fear and danger and violence. There's nothing to beat it really. My Da got drunk and wanted to do some real damage. I spent the night convincing him we'd get the stuff back in the morning. I slept on his couch.

By twelve the next day nothing had been delivered. Danny came up from Dempsey's with the word that Techno and his team were out to get us. I told him not to tell my Da.

Strangely enough Techno had a job. A good job an all. He worked in a bank and had prospects. He was a bit of a genius they said. Had Highers, the whole bit. There was a grit bin outside his house and I climbed in there six in the morning, propped the lid up with a can and sat watching. His light came on. He wandered about. His light went off and he came to the door looking great in his suit and tie and combed-back hair. He lit a fag and started walking down the hill towards me.

The last thing you expect on your way to work is a talking grit bin.

—Techno! the grit bin said.

He stopped and looked just as I jack-in-the-boxed up with a ten inch carving knife and pulled him into the bin. As he was falling I was climbing out and when his head came back up I pushed the blunt end of the blade against his neck.

—I want the fuckin stuff! Is all I said.

I took the blade away, gave him one evil stare and walked away.

By six that night the stuff was in my Maw's. Some wee ned had brung it up. Said *Techno sent this* and left. I was there when my Da handed it back to Danny. Danny was so surprised he couldn't even talk, not even to say thanks. He walked out and we could hear him tune a station up in his room. Me and my Da shook hands. Job well done.

That night I met Liam Brown in Dempsey's.

—Hear you're living in a grit bin? he said.

I laughed. He laughed.

—Fuckin jumping out the bin with a big blade!

—I had to get the stuff back.

—You never going to see through that brother of yours? Liam said.

—What d'you mean?

—Techno *bought* that stuff.

I nearly choked.

—No he never, he mugged Danny.

But even as I was saying it I knew it was true. Techno's gallousness translated now; the last thing he expected was us turning up.

I felt sick. Used. I wanted to kick the shit out of Danny. But Liam calmed me down. He'd been the same with Billy.

—There comes a day when you've got to let your brother fight his own battles, Liam said.

I should've listened to Liam.

# 2009

The doors of revenge open quiet and smooth. Billy was hiding in these flats in Airdrie. I droove up in a car I was just new after stealing and sat in the back with the windows wound slightly down to let condensation out. Two whole nights I waited and no Billy. I was starting to think he'd spotted me when there he was, looking better than I'd seen him for years. He was standing in the entrance out of the rain rolling a fag. Perfect. I took off the safety like the guy had showed me. It suddenly felt like a different object. Dropped it in my pocket and got out. I walked normal cos from this distance Billy wouldn't recognise me but just to make sure I walked with a different accent. I went round the back of the flats so I could surprise him when I turned the final corner. My plan was to push him back into the derelict area and shoot him.

—Two to the chest, the guy had said. —And once he's down, one to the head.

The rain, the high winds and the towering twelve floors made the world spin. Orange neon and the white halogen. The screams and shouts of busted lives. I focused on Danny. In hospital with tubes and

the lights and my Maw crying. And Billy slashing and
stabbing. And Danny screaming. And the blood.
I built my rage. The cunt was going to get it. Every
atom was flaring with rage as I turned the final
corner with my hand on the gun.

But I had to turn away cos Billy was talking to
a well-dressed guy who looked like a cop. I slid into
a defunct doorway. Billy and this guy, they walked
away in deep conversation to a car sitting with its
lights on. And there was somebody else in the car
I couldn't make out. Billy got in and they all shook
hands. It looked like Billy was getting introduced
to the guy in the car. Don't tell me Billy's a grass,
I was thinking. Billy Brown. The best boxer we ever
produced. A grass? They droove away and I went
back to my van. I sat thinking maybe this wasn't just
retaliation for Danny stealing Shelly and him giving
Billy a doing. This went deeper. Billy was out to get
me *through* Danny.

Billy returned about half ten. I stood in a position
where I could see the lifts and checked what floor he
stopped. The fourth. I ran outside. In the corner flat,
a light went on in the hall and bled into the living
room. Not unless that was a coincidence. But then
Billy came to the living room window, cupped his
hands and looked out. I don't know what he was
looking for but he stood staring out over the lights
of the town. Maybe he sensed there was somebody
out there. Maybe he was looking at the hospital and

thinking about Danny. I had to stop thinking about him. The more I thought of what Billy was thinking the more my anger diminished. I had to re-build my rage. I thought I seen him bless himself before he moved into the flicker of his telly.

Up I went.

His door was locked. I let the handle up slow slow oh so slow. Listened. I could hear the telly but nothing more. All the other doors on the fourth were just big metal shutters. This was where the council put junkies and alkies. The stories you heard about this place – it was like Dante's *Inferno*. Floor by floor it got worse. Even with a gun in my pocket I was wary. Listening to the numbed cacophony of scheme life I was Odysseus landing on the island of the dead. Then I remembered Billy coming into Perth all them years ago and I started wondering if I could go though with it. But my Maw's voice rang up in my head.

—Just when I thought my heart couldn't break any more, that cunt Billy Brown snaps it.

I lifted the letter box and peered through. The only light was the living room at the end of the skinny hall. Shoved my fingers through. No hanging key. I thought about kicking the door in but I didn't want to alert him. What if he had a gun? If I was in hiding I'd have a gun. Think think think. It was a Yale lock. Somebody had wrecked the doorframe around the lift. You could see down the gaps into the shaft.

I went back and tore off a bar of aluminium two feet long. I shoved it into Billy's letter box and brung it back, flattening it against the door. Angled it up at the Yale and inched it across with my fingers. I tripped the handle and the door wafted open. I had to catch it cos these flats were a vortex. I was in the lobby with the door closed and my heart pounding, mouth dry. Inching along with my back to the wall like an American cop. When I got parallel with the living room door I was watching the telly and one of Billy's bare feet. His toes were wiggling.

I listened to him laughing at *Little Britain*. And my brother lying at death's door. I burst in and kicked the telly such a whack it burst. The characters exploding out into the living room and dying on the carpet. Billy had scrambling back before he'd managed to stand up.

I pointed the gun. He held a cushion in front of him with straight arms like a shield, his head bent down behind it.

—Don't shoot, he shouted. —Don't shoot!

I grabbed his hair and pressed the gun into his nostril. I could hear his breath gushing over the end of the muzzle.

—Stevie – come on! he pleaded.

—Get on the fuckin floor, Billy!

He was on his knees pleading.

—Don't do this, he shouted.

I kicked him on the head.

—Lie down, I said, —on the fuckin floor.

I pointed the gun. But he caught my eye.

—I forgave you, remember?

—Shut it Billy.

—I fuckin forgave you.

—Shut it.

—I forgave you.

—That was different.

—How was it different?

—Cos I never fuckin meant it Billy, I said. —You did. Get on the fuckin floor.

He wouldn't move. He knelt staring into my eyes. I pointed the gun at his chest. Billy done a mad thing. He closed his eyes and started praying.

—God grant me the serenity…

—What the fuck're you doing Billy? I said.

But he kept on praying.

—… To accept the things I cannot change. Courage to change the things I can. And the wisdom to know the difference.

I tried to pull the trigger but my finger wouldn't obey. I re-aimed at his leg. Pressed it into his thigh. I couldn't even shoot him in the leg. It was all over for me violence-wise. I knew if I ever hit the drink again I'd be a washout. Whatever I'd had was gone. I'd used all my fight up gouging out a better life. That's when I realised I was crying. And Billy had the gun. But he was crying too. He took the clip out and slipped it in my left pocket, shoved the gun in my right.

—I couldn't even shoot ye Billy, I said, —I couldn't even do that.

He whipped out a serenity card.

—I'm at AA. I'm back at AA! Back at the meetings.

I hadn't noticed but his flat was full of AA stuff.

—I went to the meetings the next day. After I woke up under a tree covered in blood. When I remembered what I'd done.

He went into the kitchen. Filled the kettle. He shouted through.

—Is Danny still...?

—Critical, I said.

There was silence. I guess none of us knew what to say for a while. Then I said, —What the fuck did you do it for Billy?

He came in, sat down and flipped his palms up.

—Fuck knows. The drink? Him and Shelly?

—Me and Liam?

But he never answered that one. He just bit his lip deep.

—Let's just pray, Billy said, —to our higher powers, Stevie. Pray for Danny.

—I came here to kill you, Billy.

Billy shrugged. I repeated it.

—I came here to kill you.

—You can kill me any time, he said, —I'm not going anywhere.

I looked him in the eye. There was a clarity in those eyes that day. The same clarity I seen all those

144

years ago in Perth and for all he'd done, Billy, and all he's been through I was amazed to see he still had a soul. Then he made me laugh. He held out his hands as if he was holding a gun.

—Kill Bill, he said and laughed. —Kill Bill!

He kept saying it over and over and we laughed like two wee boys in a canoe. In the rapids of living we were, me and Billy. The danger and exhilaration of unforeseen rocks and currents. White water and the promise of peace. Future rivers, still and dark. We soared along on the rush of just being. The carnival of life. Me and Billy.

—Kill Bill, we were shouting, —kill Bill!

When we stopped laughing we knelt and prayed for Danny, had a cup of tea and talked about the regeneration of the soul. I was looking out the window most of the time. It was a peace descended upon us. That house that one night was a holy point in the universe. In there sins didn't count, our souls were temporarily cleansed and we had a glimpse of how it might be – in this life or the next. We communicated so we did me and Billy. We pure communicated. Clarity.

There's a Buddhist practice called Metta Bhavana. It's when you generate a core of love in yourself and emanate it outwards to everybody and everything. That's what I was doing out over the lights of Lanarkshire. Sending out the love that had somehow come out of the darkness and the thing was, the more I poured out the more it came cascading in. And I realised that's where God lived, not in the light but in the darkness. He didn't care who you were or what you'd done. You could be forgiven, you could be loved. I turned to face Billy. He was first. He held his arms out. I went over and we hugged.

—What happened to you Billy? I said. —You were the best boxer that ever came out of this town.

—Same as what happened to you. Same as what happened to every fuckin one of us – booze.

When I left Billy that night something left me. Left my body, left my soul. And I think I know what it was; hope singing its triumph and sadness fleeing away. I lobbed the gun into a skip and flung the clip in the canal and by the time I got back to my Maw's to tell them I couldn't do it things had changed. My Maw was happy and singing. Danny had regained consciousness. He was getting better. I told my Maw I couldn't find Billy.

—Maybe just as well son.

My Da was drunk listening to country and western. And singing. I told him I couldn't find Billy. But he could see it in my eyes.

—You're a fuckin liar, he said. —You couldn't do it could ye?

I hung my head.

—Give me the gun. I'll do it, he said. —I'm old. It doesn't matter about me any more.

I told him I flung the gun in the canal and tried to explain about Billy but he shook his head.

—That's your brother up there in that hospital.

He wanted revenge.

—What about fuckin forgiveness? I shouted as I stormed out. I heard him shout back as I left the house.

—Forgiveness? Forgiveness is for nuns, he said.

—And poofs.

# January 1999

Six months after we got the sack I was hitting the drink something awful. I told Danny I had to get off it. He tried to persuade me but I was serious. He had Billy to drink with by then anyway. Drink's got a way of making enemies friends and friends enemies. I had my last drink on the Monday, I'd sobered up by Tuesday, horrors started on the Wednesday and it was a week of shakes and sweats and guilt and remorse before the paranoia slipped away.

It was a couple of days before I could lose myself again in a book and a couple of days more before I could open the living room blinds. I got a fright cos the houses across the road were nearly finished. When light flooded into the living room there was a DVD on the floor. I couldn't remember stealing it. *Amélie* it was called.

Another week passed without a drop and I was thinking maybe I didn't have a drink problem. I decided to conduct an experiment.

I went round to Tabs and got a gram of dope and bought six cans out Asda. I was tempted to buy twelve but then the experiment would fall apart. It was late January and there had been snow on the ground for over a week. It was turned to a muddy slush outside my flat by lorries building the private estate.

I closed the blinds and unplugged the phone, locked the doors and put out the lights, rolled four joints, sat them like miniature mummies on the table and had myself a shower savouring a night mellowed out watching the DVD. I put on baggy jogging bottoms and a t-shirt too big for me. In the mirror I could've been anybody. One of them guys you see on adverts for cars. They get out their bed on a Sunday morning, slip into baggy clothes and go to the shop. The newsvendor always waves at them. They come home to a boiling percolator and sip it on the balcony overlooking a canal. Then we see their car and it's a silver Volkswagen or Audi. Tonight I was going to be civilised. Normal. Just a guy, happy in his own company, staying in for the night. Not getting drunk. Just a social drinker.

I got one of the cans out the fridge and put it in position. I'd spent the day tidying and cleaning and hoovering. As much to keep the blues at bay as anything. But it felt good to be clean and tidy and I was getting more relaxed by the minute. Even better, the street outside used to be a racing track for neds going from this scheme to the next but they blocked it off when they started building. Only cars now were the odd neighbour. Or taxis. I settled in, opened the can and took the first cold slug. Let it fizz in my belly and its cold tentacles creep out. When it reached my fingers I lifted a joint and lit up.

Had a few puffs and stuck the DVD in. At first
I thought *fuckin subtitles – great!* But it drew me
in and I soon forgot about subtitles. It was about a
girl called Amélie. And I kind of identified with her.
If I was French and she was real and we lived in
the same bit of Paris we'd be in love. She looked
like she would understand me. And she was beautiful
but nobody seemed to notice. She had a soul the
size of a planet and nocunt noticed that either.
She was searching for something and by the time
I'd smoked two joints and drank two cans we were
searching thegether. Me and Amélie. Sometimes
I couldn't tell the film from reality. And another
thing; I left school with a dinner ticket and that's
all and even though I've read a squillion books they
were all English. If ever I knew any French I'd forgot
that I knew it. But here I was, understanding everything. I didn't read the subtitles. Dope makes that
kind of effort impossible. Getting the third can out
the fridge was momentous. I walked backwards,
keeping my eyes on the screen. I was in love.
Honestly. If Amélie walked in my door I wouldn't
have been shocked. When I crashed the third can
everything seemed possible. I looked at the door.
It was ominous. It was glowing. Buzzing like it was
light rather than the wood. Behind it was this
colourful Paris. It would swing out into Abbesses
Métro and she'd be on her bench. She'd get up and
walk towards me as our train arrived on a gush of
Métropolitain air. We'd kiss and she'd lift one heel.

We'd get on the train and disappear into that tunnel. Forever.

But where was I? Here was the film. I was back in the room and here was the film. I lit the third joint. Amélie was working in a bar and two people were shagging in the toilets. All the bottles and glasses shook and rattled. Amélie tilted her head and smiled and in the Louvre, The Mona Lisa was probably falling off the wall in envy. Paris couldn't handle two beautiful enigmas. I'm on my knees now close to the telly and she's looking at me. She's about to say *je t'aime* when I heard people crunching on the street with a tone that told me it had been snowing again. And I knew they were coming to me. I put the joint out and lifted one blind slat. The world was white blotches falling and the lights from the motorway silhouetting the houses. Footprints through the car park and into the close. I couldn't right see who it was. I turned the DVD off and sat with my back to the wall but I was sure they could hear my breathing. I slid closer. Heard feet scratching on the doormat. It wouldn't be the cops. They'd've done three big bangs by now. The letter box lifted up. I pulled my feet in.

—Stevie! Ye there? It's Danny.

His hair was an amazing white. Billy the gauze ghost Brown was with him looking like somebody had threw a net curtain over him. Billy's wife had flung him out and him and Danny were on a bender.

—Where's these fireplaces? Danny said.

—What?

—The Adams fireplaces? said Billy. —Where are they?

They were needing money for drink. I closed the door and watched their boots leave a black cold stain of damp like big thick exclamation marks on my clean carpet. Billy started telling me Liam was getting out the jail soon.

—Won't be too pleased when he finds out yous two're running about thegether, I said.

But Billy had news for me.

—He says when he gets out the jail you're a dead man, said Billy. —No offence like Stevie; tell that cunt Stevie he's a dead man he said.

—Fuckin shut up about that Billy, we're here for the fireplace, said Danny.

I opened a blind.

—See they houses there?

They did.

—The first three have got fireplaces in them.

—How d'you know? said Billy.

I showed him the big yellow tick in the living room window. It meant the house had been inspected and was ready for the owner to move in.

—And when do they move in? Danny wanted to know.

I shrugged. Could be in the morning or a month. All depended. Sometimes they'd move in as soon as their big tick went up, were there that night in a big furniture van. Danny wanted to know if there was any more houses near completion but he couldn't say completion and I realised he was drunk. I told him nothing coming up to that stage as far as I could see. He sat on the edge of the couch but missed and went straight onto the floor banging his head. I laughed and Billy laughed. We were laughing that much me and Billy we had to hold each other up. Danny got up laughing too with that sparkle in his eye, rubbed his head and said, —Well big fullah, It seems as if the deed'll have to be done the night.

He looked out the blinds. His big skinny hands crumpling three or four instead of sliding one up.

—That one there? he said.

—Aye.

—With the big yellow tick? Billy said.

—Big yellow tick.

—Right, he said, —keep the edge up. Hear anything start flashing your living room light on and off.

I agreed and we went out to the close door. They didn't feel the cold but it hit me. The snow was still falling and the more it fell the quieter it got. I noticed they'd no transport and asked just how they planned getting this Adams fireplace away considering it would weigh about two hundredweight. What I really meant was – you're not using my van. He winked with a big Danny know-all wink and told me he'd parked a knocked-off van across the railway line. He wasn't so daft as to drive right up the street. And off they went with the swagger of master criminals; two eejit alkies in the snow.

I got in and put my living room light out. I went to the blinds to keep the edge up. Cops could come any minute and they'd be lifted. Jailed. Then I thought of Liam saying I was a dead man and it made me angry Danny and Billy bringing that kind of bad news to my door. Especially when I was conducting my experiment. Fuck them, I thought. Fuck them all. Fuck Liam and fuck Danny and fuck Billy! Fuck the white Adams fireplace. What about Amélie? I let the blind fall on Danny and Billy like a guillotine and put *Amélie* back on. She finds another photo under the photo-booth in the Metropolitan. She was that beautiful and so lonely. We were made for each other and I made up my mind to get a cheap Ryanair to Paris soon as I got a few quid thegether. There must be other, real, Amélies in Paris.

There was this almighty crash. I went to the window and could see nothing. I peered through snowflakes. The big yellow tick was gone and in its place a ragged hole where the window used to be. A wooden pallet lay on the snow under a shower of glass. I realised they'd threw that at the window to get in. I mean – what about going round the back and forcing open a window? Or kicking a door in? Not these two drunken bastards. My heart was thumping. Surely somecunt had phoned the cops? I watched but nothing stirred. Then more crashing. And swearing. Danny was shouting at the top of his voice.

—Come off ya fireplace bastard, he was shouting.

155

Amélie was talking to somebody in French. I sat back down but I'd lost my concentration. I re-lit the second-last joint. But I couldn't get mellow again. I was getting paranoid in fact. So I put it out. There was bumping and grunting coming over the snow and I wished I hadn't answered the door. Or at least that they'd get the fireplace and get to fuck. My blood pressure was sky high when I heard four big thumps at the door. I let them in and Danny grinned. Billy took a swig from a Buckie bottle.

—Can't get the fuckin thing off the wall, Danny said.

—So I heard!

—Was we loud? said Billy.

I looked at him as if he was mad.

—It'll be screwed on with two screws, I said. — Near the top. One at each side.

—Seen them, said Danny.

—Well, did you not screw them off?

—With what? said Billy and handed Danny a slug at the Buckie.

They hadn't even brung a screwdriver. Anything. My experiment was ruined but I had two cans and one and a half joints left. If I could get rid of them I could salvage something. But fuck! There was blood on the floor. A lot, and when I traced it back to Danny there was big blots coming out of his jacket sleeve.

—Danny you've got blood coming out your sleeve.

He looked up the wrong sleeve then the right

one. His hand was like a red rubber glove. He liked to act tough so he gave me a puzzled look like he was looking for, say, a tear in his jacket. He found it. It was a deep gouge in the shape of a triangle just above his hand. Three inches each side – an equilateral – two sides blood and fat and one side skin. He lifted it like a hinge to inspect it. Blood was pumping out with every heartbeat.

—I knew I cut myself going in there, he said. —Have you got a screwdriver?

I don't know if he was acting hard or really was going back in. And I didn't ask. I wrapped a tea towel round his arm. The blood was sticky on my bare feet and I cursed the cunt. Billy spotted Amélie in the living room.

—Who's the babe? he said.

I never answered him. I just twisted the tea towel until the blood stopped.

—Hold that Billy, till I get my shoes, I said.

Billy held it, watching Amélie go about her business.

—Is that a porno? Billy was shouting. —It looks like a porno. Bet she'd give ye some blow job with lips like that. Bet she's only fifteen.

It was making me angry but I had to get Danny to hospital. It wasn't that serious but if he went back to the pub or the fireplace he could lose too much blood. I hid the cans at the back of the fridge and asked Billy to wait there. Watch out for the cops.

—I'll have a wank, he said. —To Amélie.

And I hoped he was kidding.

Outside there was a trail of blood right up to my close. If the cops did come they were coming right to me. I wanted to punch Danny. I got him in my van. I don't know how it started. It hadn't been on the road since the tax and insurance ran out. But I was thinking if we got stopped I could show then Danny's bloody arm.

I managed to obliterate some big pink blotches of blood as I reversed out. The snow was thick and crinkly under the wheels and there was hardly any cars out there. Even the main roads were five inches in snow. He asked if I wanted a swig of his Buckie. I was proud of myself for refusing.

—Suit yourself then, he said and downed the lot and burped and laughed and shouted *yee ha!* When I braked at the hospital the snow on the roof slid onto the windscreen and plunged us into darkness. Danny got out singing and I guided him into Casualty. He took great pride in showing the hinged cut to the nurses but they were unperturbed. They took his details and asked us to wait. I listened to that skinny bastard's drivel for three hours before he was seen. I went in with him. It was a good-looking doctor in her thirties. A bit ravaged by time and work but still sexy. But the main thing about her was she looked sad. Sadness was coming out of her pores. I could actually feel it. I thought she had a thing for me but I couldn't be sure. I liked her white overall. I think she only had her underwear on beneath. She

kept asking what happened. Danny made up this
story about falling on a bottle but she never believed
him and when he refused anaesthetic she didn't
flinch and sewed his arm up like a rag doll for a
child. She took to talking to me as she worked cos he
was making no sense at all. And bursting into song
now and then saying *Eh* to her and winking.

—Eh!?

Wink.

I told her I was his brother. That he turned up out
of the blue covered in blood. I was watching a film.

—Which film?

—*Amélie*, and she said it was a great film. Her
opinion of me went up on the strength of that one
film. I was thinking about asking her out. But then
my inner voice was saying *you and a doctor? Are you
mad? She'll have you carted off to Carstairs.* Her
hands were soft and delicate and her eyes were
heartbreaking. I could smell a faint trace of yesterday's perfume and sweat. When we left she said
*enjoy the film* and I said I would. Our eyes met for a
second and I'm sure she wanted me to say something
else, or she wanted to say something but Danny
screamed *yee ha* and when I turned back she was
walking up a lonely corridor.

The wind buffeted the van all the way home.
When we got back to my close at midnight the snow
had been steadily falling and there wasn't a trace of
blood. I got out and said, —I'm going to my bed
Danny. Do you need me to drive you home?

He shook his head and asked for a screwdriver.

—What?

—Have ye got one of them star screwdrivers?

—You're fuckin kidding?

—No! I'm not going home without that fireplace.

I looked at him, at his bandaged arm, his rubber drunk face. There was only one way I was going to get peace. I took him in and sat him on the couch beside a sleeping Billy, gave him one of my cans and went out into the howling wind. It was practically a blizzard now. Nobody could hear a thing. I picked every jagged shard from the window and when I was finished it looked like a big dark pane of glass. I checked for eyes as best I could through the snow and climbed in. It was a fuckin mess. Danny and Billy had been kicking holes in the plasterboard around the fireplace. Ripped out some four by twos. They'd caused thousands of pounds of damage. The wall would need replaced but the fireplace was minted. Unscrewing it was a five-minute job. I dragged it to the window, lifted one leg out then slid it along and tilted the other leg out. The snow was good. Once it got going on its mantlepiece I pushed that fireplace like a sledge. Now and then it ploughed in and I had to jiggle it free, slope it up, and push again. I was careful at the railway, turning it on its feet and walking it across. At the other end, sure enough, was an old Astra van. The owner was probably glad it had been stole. It was open and the keys were in the ignition. I got the fireplace in and went back for the hearth. Before I got out I scanned the room and thought of the poor bastards in the morning. It would have to be yellow ticked all over again. I got the hearth in the van and locked the door.

When I got back Danny and Billy were snoring. I shook them and said time to go home. They asked to stay the night but I wanted that last can and one and a half joints to myself. I wanted a little bit of peace. I wasn't going to bed until I had that. I got them out and over the railway, into the van and their seatbelts on. It was two in the morning and not a soul about but just to make him more alert I shoved a handful of snow down Danny's back. He screamed and woke fully up. He turned and looked at the white Adams fireplace in the back.

—Thanks brother. I owe you one, he said.

—So you do, I said.

Billy winked. Danny *yee haa'd* and droove off flinging up snow. When I got back I locked the doors, closed the blinds, lit a joint, got rid of Billy's wank wrapped in white toilet paper, opened a can and pressed play.

Amélie was in an underground station waiting for me but no matter how I tried I couldn't get that old feeling back. It wasn't the same. I turned it off and went to the window. I wondered what that doctor was doing right now. All footprints to my door had been obliterated.

# Autumn 2004

When I was in Perth I took to reading. A lot. There was a drive on to improve literacy and I was their good example. Every week or two I'd sign a consent for a photo of me sitting reading for *The Inside News* or some literary classic. For that they gave me a wee job in the library. I loved it. I'd always been a reader but now, with so much time on my hands, I devoured book after book. Education tried to get me to do an OU degree. They wanted me to wear it as a badge of rehabilitation. And even though they meant well there was an unspoken rubric beneath that. And it was this:

> In order to become a better person, you have to take on middle class values; when you become like them they feel safe.

The stories and the articles in the papers always sent out the same message: here's a guy becoming a bet-ter person by educating himself. But that wasn't why I was reading. I was reading cos I loved stories. I read all sorts of books and poetry and stuff. Ancient Greeks and all that. I loved the strong-willed hero. And I loved words. I loved words from everywhere and anywhere. The more words you had the safer you were cos when the words stop the violence

starts. Whether it's the violence you do to others,
or the violence you do to yourself.

This day and it was just me and Sof, the screw.
He was quieter than usual and I thought he must be
worrying about something at home. I was reading
*The Odyssey* and was right into it so his silence suited
me. It was the bit where Odysseus was on the raft
and it was just water everywhere and Poseidon was
smashing the sea with his fists and even though he
was wee bit of a blowhard, Odysseus, you still kinda
felt sorry for him. Anyway, all that water made me
want to piss.

—Going for a piss, Sof, I said. He waved me on.
He had a strange look on his face.

The library was like a long wide corridor really.
The toilets away at the back. I thought I heard
something when I was in. I stopped the flow and
could've swore I heard Sof leaving but he wasn't
allowed to leave you on your own.

When I got out was I shocked to see Billy Brown
standing in the middle of the library. Stunned to a
lump of wood I was.

—Billy! I sputtered out.

And I instinctively put my hands on the back of a
chair, ready to crack him one with it.

—Leave it, Billy said, —I just want to talk.

He had a funny look about him that day. He was
shining, pink and radiant. And his body language
had an accent of peace. One thing for sure: he
wasn't going to attack me. My mind was doing over

time. Had he got banged up? But no. He had civvies on. We all wore the dark blue SPS Perth sweat tops. How the fuck did he get in here? And furthermore – what the fuck was he doing in here?

—D'you want a coffee? I said.

—Aye, fling us one on.

I made him a coffee and we had some small chat about who I was dubbed with and all that. Then I had to ask him.

—Billy, how the fuck did you get in here?

—AA, he said.

—AA?

—Aye, there's a meeting in the Learning Centre every Thursday at two.

But that still puzzled me. What the fuck's Billy got to do with AA? He seen that question in my eyes.

—I'm a year sober, he said, —next Friday.

—Fuck sake Billy! I was genuinely delighted for him. I told him well done and shook his hand but I was still puzzling how he got in the fuckin library.

—How the fuck did you get in here but Billy? The library?

—Sof's AA an all, Billy said.

—But he's risking his job letting you in here.

—I know.

There was a pause. We sipped our coffee. There was a noise outside and I knew Sof was there and I knew he'd be nervous. I wondered why he was risking his job. What did he have to gain? What did Billy have to gain? I was starting to get paranoid.

Like I was losing my mind. Then I sensed something about Billy. Here was a man who wanted to say something but couldn't get it out. He'd look from his coffee now and then and his mouth would fall open but nothing would come out.

—So what is it? I said to Billy.

Billy looked nervous.

—Come on Billy, you don't walk into a library in the middle of Perth Prison for a coffee and a chat about the weather. Is it Danny? Is there something wrong with Danny?

Billy shook his head no and looked me direct in the eye.

—I've come to forgive you, he said.

There was a white flash. Bang. It was like a punch in the face. I don't know where it came from. Then this flash ran right through my body and it seemed to be cleaning me. It's hard to explain but it was like the way a scanner or a photocopier runs down a sheet of paper shining its light straight through and by the time it hit my toes I was crying. Billy came over, stood me up and hugged me.

—You were only trying to protect your brother, he said.

And he forgave me. Up to then I didn't realise that forgiveness was an actual *thing*, an act that can be performed. Billy looked straight in my eyes and said it.

—Stevie, I forgive you, he said.

He kissed me on the forehead and let me hold onto

him cos by now I was crying. I was going to be in that jail for a long time still but that one wee bit of forgiveness went a long way down the line.

I eventually looked up and could see his blurred outline through the tears. I wanted to say *thanks Billy* but it wouldn't come out. I was choking on the release of guilt and remorse.

—D'you want to go to the meeting? Billy asked.

—What meeting?

—The AA meeting.

—Who, me?

—You might find it interesting.

I had to go, didn't I?

—Aye. Alright Billy, I said.

Sof came in.

—Stevie wants to go to the meeting, Billy said.

Sof took us to the Learning Centre locking every door behind. Every time taking Billy closer to the outside and reminding me of my sentence. I was thinking *what the fuck am I doing going to an AA meeting?* There's no way I was an alcoholic.

But after it I wasn't too sure. I wasn't too sure at all. The guy speaking had done a lot of the same things I'd done. But he wasn't doing them any more, he said. And he was happy. Had peace of mind. And you could see he was telling the truth. When it was finished Billy gave me a big fat blue book. Of all the books in my life, and I didn't know it at the time, this would be the most important. It was called *Alcoholics Anonymous.*

Back in my cell that night I flicked through it. There was a bit highlighted in yellow highlighting pen:

But what about the real alcoholic? He may start off as a moderate drinker; he may or may not become a continuous hard drinker; but at some stage of his drinking career he begins to lose all control of his liquor consumption, once he starts to drink. Here is a fellow who has been puzzling you, especially in his lack of control. He does absurd, incredible, tragic things while drinking. He is a real Dr Jekyll and Mr Hyde.

Billy had wrote below it – *see you next week*. Even though I hadn't drank since I got in the jail, I was going to soon as I got out. I was smoking dope and taking whatever I could get in there. I went along to the meeting the next week eager to see Billy and tell him something in that book had touched me. But no Billy. This guy talked about being clean and sober and clean meant drugs. Do nothing to evade the truth. He was addicted to a new drug now this guy; reality.

Billy had stumbled me into a programme that would make me a better person without becoming middle class. I asked if any of them had spoke to him recently. Things went quiet. There was a bad feeling.
—What?

Billy went back on the drink a day before his first birthday.

Once I got a couple of years behind me in AA I began to see the tragedy of my life. I'd lean on the table reading that big book and I'd get to thinking about my past and the tears of regret, the tears of guilt, would well up. Every day for seven years I sat at the window looking to where I thought home must be. I bleached a white stain deep into that table. Right through to the grain.

Sometimes I'd lie on my bunk and imagine I was on a raft, the sea going out everywhere and I'd float away. Every part of me free from that jail except my body. Sometimes, half asleep, half awake, I'd see an island indistinct through mist. And even though I'd never seen an island in my life, except for on the telly and in books, I knew that island was home. That's where I was heading.

# Spring 2005

It wasn't long after Billy came to see me in Perth that he got the jail. I heard it was police assault, that he'd lifted his hands to his wife again. She was in a bad state and when she came to Billy was in bed and she called the cops. When they crashed in Billy sprang up and laid into them. Naked. And he was laying into them when they dragged him to the van. Still naked. Broke both their noses, I heard. His wife was flinging all his stuff off the veranda.

—Don't come fuckin back, she was shouting.
—You're a bastard. A right sick rotten bastard!

She had their daughter held to her side and they were both crying. A police doctor went in and guys in white paper suits. They were really going for Billy this time. The cops pulled into Hannah's scrap yard on their way to the station, ostensibly to let Billy put his clothes on. But they dragged him onto the ash and gave him a helluva kicking. I heard he got five years and wondered if he'd end up in Perth.

But he didn't. It was Peterhead. I thought about writing but you get caught up in routine in the jail and time gets behind you and pushes you on.

A year after Billy got the jail this guy, Wires, landed down in Perth from Peterhead. He was a bit of a reader and we got talking in the library. He asked me all the questions. What jails had I been in? What kind of sentences had I had? What was I in for now? He'd've knew that from the other cons. But it was always respect to ask. As I told him what happened I could see Wires was troubled.

—That's it, I said when I'd finished, —just a night went wrong on the drink.

— Billy Brown?

—Hey that's right, I said. —Did you come across him in Peterhead?

Wires looked at me as if I'd insulted his granny.

—What? I said.

—What the fuck would I be doing in with the beasts?

—Beast? Billy's not a beast, I said.

—Billy Brown? Ex-boxer? Worked on the building sites?

—Aye.

—He's a fuckin beast. I pished in his tea daily man. Wanked in his soup.

I was sure Wires was wrong.

—Wait a minute. I knew Billy. He was a lot of things but he was no beast.

—Stevie, says Wires, —ye can never tell a beast. They're not always fat scoutmasters with specs ye know. Sometimes they're the last cunts ye expect.

—It was polis assault Billy got done for. Five years he got.

—Who told ye that?

—Can't remember. Some remand guy that was in here a year ago.

—He'd be a beast an all.

—What? The remand guy?

—Aye, said Wires. —They always stick up for each other they bastards. Ye never get the truth out them. They're sick. They only tell the truth to each other. For fuckin kicks.

I sat down trying to compute how Billy could be a paedo and me knowing him all these years. Not a hint. All right, we all knew he lifted his hands to his wife when he was full of the drink but truth be told we'd all done that. That's the reason my wife flung me out. It was the frustration of being a boy in a man's body that caused the trouble. Sometimes the only answer was to lash out. Wires spun a chair round and sat on it. Told me as if the whole jail might be listening.

—That Billy guy, he gave his wife a hiding. Knocked her out. Fractured skull. And when she was out for the count on the carpet he took his daughter in the room.

—No Wires!

—He took his daughter into the room and raped her.

—No. Not Billy.

—Listen Stevie, my mate seen the charge sheet. He took her in the room. Twelve she was. Raped her. But somebody had phoned the polis when they heard the wife screaming. Okay, so they take ages

to come. The wife's just wakening up on the floor.
They burst into the room and there's Billy naked in
bed sleeping; with his daughter right beside him
quivering with terror.

—Fuck sake!

It's all I could say. My jaw was open and I stared at
the floor.

—Billy!?

Wires nodded.

—A beast?

—Sorry to burst your bubble mate.

The books were spinning. I could hardly breathe.
I shouted over to Sof.

—Going for a piss, Sof.

—Okay Stevie.

I went in there and retched and retched. When I
got out Wires had made me a coffee.

—Get that down your neck, he said.

# 1999

Billy told Danny me and him better stay out Liam's road the day and went in to meet him.

—Anything happens I've got to take Liam's side, Billy said. —Yous know the score.

We did. Danny asked Billy to keep Liam out of Dempsey's.

—That's the first place he'll want to look Billy, Danny said. —But you tell him we're not that daft to be hanging about in there.

But that night, when they came into Dempsey's, me and Danny ducked down laughing; with nerves mostly. Liam and Billy were like meercats stretching up over the crowd looking for us. Billy made eye contact but never let on to Liam. I got on all fours and crawled along among the legs. Unusual things weren't unusual in Dempsey's so nobody said nothing. Danny followed and we sniggered and crawled behind the bar.

—What the fuck're yous up to? Annie Kerr whispered down out the side of her mouth.

I said *shht* and we made our way out the back door. As I closed it Liam and Billy were ordering drinks. Liam asked Annie if she'd seen the Dolans. She looked about the bar for us.

Outside our laughter came out in clouds. We got a

carry-out from Haddows and went up the chinkee's close. Two Buckie and four cans. It was cold except for the kitchen grill throwing out evaporated chicken curries and sweet and sour Hong Kong style. Danny took a long gourmet sniff.

—Can't you just can smell those seagulls, he said in a posh voice.

—Best seagull this side of the Luggie burn, I said, —and they do a mean cat an all.

We made our mind up to get a seagull cashew nuts and black crow curry later.

—Flied lice, Danny said.

We drank and done all the chinkee jokes. *The sore finger. The Rubber Chicken. Watch the wall. Yous all look the same to me*. Then me and him got talking about old times. The time I found him drunk when he was six, prising the glasses off the table.

—I don't remember that. he said.

—No fuckin wonder – you were steaming, I went and he laughed. And I laughed. When we stopped we had our backs against the heater looking up through our own rising breath.

There was stars.

The top of my body was warm but from the arse down was frozen and our feet kept slipping outwards on the ice. One of us would fall suddenly and the other would drag him upright. And the more we drank the more we slipped. That close was exotic food smells and cold air and laughter echoing. And me and Danny.

Then.

Voices.

—Shh, I said.

Yup – voices right enough it was. And they were arguing about money. Old bad money and me and Danny knew the exact amount. When they came up me and Danny says *alright* like we were expecting them.

—We've been looking everywhere for yous, Billy said, walking a line between Liam and Danny.

—Did ye find us? said Danny, laughing through his nose.

—We've fuckin found ye now ya cheeky cunt, said Liam. Liam turned his attention to me.

—I done seven months for you ya cunt, he said, and he moved at me but Billy was holding him back.

—D'ye want to end up banged up again? Billy said and the way he said it we knew he'd been saying that to Liam all night. He'd already took the edge off the rage Liam had been nursing in jail.

—Ye never done seven months for me Liam, I said.

—What!

—Ye done it cos ye attacked the gaffer.

He was spitting rage now, Liam.

—Aye cos you ripped us off!

—You concreted the outside of the pans! Danny shouted.

—Who's talking to you ya fuckin jakie?

—Me. Ya fuckin glass-jawed two round cabbage.

It was getting het up fast. Billy was holding Liam back by the jacket.

—I'll break that giant beak of yours, rat boy.

—I'll fuckin rat boy ye, said Danny and went right up to Liam.

Billy tried to cool the beans.

—Look, he said with his palm out, —just give us the money back. That'll settle it, nat right Liam?

I knew that would never settle it. Liam had murder in his eye. So to buy some time I asked Billy why they never tried to get the money off Sterling instead of laying into the gaffer.

—Aye, and he'd've gave us it, said Billy.

—He gave us it, I said.

—Cos you whipped the fuckin ethics out on him, said Billy, —Danny told me.

—You and your fuckin big words, said Liam.

He was a lot drunker than Billy. He leaned in and lifted a finger at me.

—Know what? I'm going to stuff all your fancy patter up your arse!

—That'll be a bit hard Liam, I said. —There's already ten pints of lager, two Curly wurlys, three bottles of Buckfast and twenty Lambert and Butler up there – and that's just this week!

Danny laughed.

—Ya bastard! Liam screamed and lunged at me.

But this time Danny yanked him back and banged him against the heated grill. They were two dark shapes in the steam. Liam pulled his arm back to punch Danny but his elbow hit the metal and he screamed. Danny stuck the head on him with an almighty thud, Liam's head was swimming in stars

and spices as he slid down. The chinkee cook was
shouting in Cantonese. But that thing in Liam, that
thing he'd been nurturing in jail, that ball of white
rage made him spring up and rain automatic blows
in Danny's direction. A few caught Danny as he
skipped backwards impersonating a boxer.

—Float like a butterfly, sting like a bee, said Danny
in a Muhammad Ali accent.

Liam turned his consciousness full on, switched his
drunkenness off and went at Danny. I moved and
Billy grabbed me.

—Square jig, Billy said. And I leaned back.

But it was an ice rink and they skidded and slipped.
Punched themselves into pirouettes. Danny never
landed a blow. Then Liam got him in the corner. It
was two to the head four to the body and Danny
folded like wet newspaper. He was on the ground in
the foetal position shouting.

—I give in. I've had enough. I've had enough.

But Liam started putting the boot in. Vicious.
I lunged forwards leaving Billy behind. Liam heard
me and was turning when I caught him this holy
crack on the jaw. Down he went, his feet going one
way and his head the other. Sparkled. Liam dinked
his skull off the corner of the heater as he went.

It was an eerie thump when he hit the ground.
Danny was about to lay the boot in but he seen
something was wrong. So did Billy.

—Liam! Billy screamed, falling to his knees beside
his brother.

We knew he was dead. His eyes were open but they were departed eyes. The smell of curry bled everywhere and the chinkee was shouting and banging the grill. Billy held his hand up. His finger was covered in blood.

—There's a big hole in the back of his head, Billy said. —A big hole. My finger went right in it.

The blood came slow and steady. That's when I kicked Billy full in the face.

—For fuck sake! Danny said and was about to attack me when I pointed.

Billy's blade was lying on the ground. I stood on it. Billy looked up.

—He's dead, Billy said. —You've killed him.

Danny started crying. And we ran. By The Fountain I was away from Danny and I kept going till I was a mile down the canal.

# Echo

I remember what it was – we were off to buy
another Bruce Springsteen album. I'd turned Joe onto
The Boss. I was doing everything I could to make up
for all the years I wasn't there. Me and him had
made good progress this past wee while. It was good
to be walking along the main street with my son and
I was off to Barcelona that night with Penelope. She
was ten years older than me but still beautiful inside
and outside. I was going to Woolies closing down
sale to pick up a few last-minute things.

Joe seen Billy Brown in the distance and nudged
me.

—There's that guy Billy, said Joe.

I was trying to avoid him even though I'd heard he
was back at the meetings. But before I could do anything Joe shouted him over.

—Billy!

That's when I seen he was steaming. He was two
steps forward, another one forward for good luck
and one to the side. Any side. Carrier bags pulling
him down like anchors. The bus swerved onto the
kerb to miss him as he staggered across. The bags
swung out and hit me on the legs as his big red face
shuffled its features. I realised I could've got away cos
he was only beginning to recognise me.

—Aww! All right big fullah, he says so the whole main street turns round. He grabbed me and held onto me. He was stinking of Buckfast and pish. The bags hit me behind the knees and I could feel the lice jumping from his hair to mine.

—I heard you were off the drink Billy? Back at the meetings?

He un-hugged me and gave me a face between apology and defeat. Offered me a can of Super. I was off it ten years but I didn't want to rub it in or put Billy down. He offered one to Joe. Joe just screwed his face up politely. I wanted away from there.

—They're doing Bruce Springsteen for a quid in Woolies, I said.

♫ I come from down in the valley, sang Billy. Loud. —where mister when you're young. They bring you up to do like your daddy done...

My body was leaning away in case he got to the chorus. But he stopped abruptly, holding one finger in front of his face.

— Your Danny's up the chinkee's close.

I looked at him with a big *what?* on my face.

—Danny and Shelly. This is our cargo. They're up the chinkee's close.

Shit! If I don't go up Billy'll say – seen your Stevie and his son on the main street. Danny'll ask if he told me he was there. Billy'll say aye and I'll be all the cunts. I didn't want to go up. Anything can happen up closes. Then I thought – ach! What's the harm in chewing the fat with my young brother for a couple of minutes?

Up we go through the reverberation of our own footsteps. The light and sounds of the main street fading.

Shelly's a beached whale with dyed blonde hair.
She's sitting on the wall and I swear the wall was
bending underneath her. She's not right the lassie.
She was pregnant for two and a half years once.
Told my Maw and sisters she was two months and as
time went by she kept on saying she was overdue,
the doctor said it would definitely be in the next
week.

—Anytime now Annie, she'd say to my Maw.
It was hard to tell if she was pregnant or not so at
first nobody was suspicious. But once she was twelve
months we started to click. After that my Maw and
sisters just humoured her. Is that right hen? Aw that's
a sin. Can they not do anything for you? Bring you
on? Something like that?

—I've to go in next week Annie, she'd say. —
They're going to seduce me. But nobody laughed.
It was a liberty to laugh at her.

—Look who's here! Billy says and Danny turns at
an impossible angle. His scars were healing up nicely.
His right arm is crooked out in front of him and a can
of Super swings from his thumb and middle finger,

—Danny look who it is! Look who it is! Shelly's
shouting.

—For what *hic* do we owe the honour! Danny
says. —For what do we owe the honour! *Hic*.

He came and flung his arms round me. By this time
Joe was pressed against the wall, watching. He'd

slipped into a parallel universe without noticing.
This one.

—Must be a special occasion. That's all I can say –
must be a special occasion, Shelly's saying as Danny
cries all over me.

Sobbing so much I could feel his chest pounding
off mine and his back going up and down like a boned
balloon. And d'you know what was going through
my head? Not his tears. Cos you can never trust the
tears of an alky. The only thing they're sincere about
is where their next drink's coming from. What was
going through my head was – I hope he doesn't spill
that beer on me. If he does I'll stink of alcohol. I'll
have to walk along the main street. People'll smell it
and think I'm back on the drink. In this town it'll only
be a matter of hours before my Maw starts worrying
about me all over again. But then I thought – he's an
alcoholic, he's not going to spill a drop. He's got the
can in a mechanically sound pivot between his thumb
and middle finger. The beer stays parallel to gravity
as the can goes every which way. So I let him cuddle
me safe in the knowledge that he'd not spill a drop.
In the background Shelly was still talking. I couldn't
really hear at first cos Danny was shouting.

—Shut it you. This is my brother come to visit me.
Keep your mouth shut!

But she keeps on going and that's when I hear
what she's saying.

—I want a cuddle, Shelly sobs, —I want a cuddle.

At first I think she's taking the piss but when

Danny breaks off to slap her in the face I see she's deadly serious. She does want a cuddle.

—What did I tell you? says Danny and slaps her. The slap echoes round the place. Its ring diminishing with the increasing pain.

—Fuck sake Danny, says Billy and pulls him back.

Danny punches Billy full force on the chest and Billy reels onto his arse looking up at me.

—Leave it Billy, I say. Billy nods okay.

—I only wanted a cuddle, Shelly says, —I was only asking him for a cuddle.

Danny lifts his hand again and I grab it. He was never very strong and I always was. So I pulled him gently back and went over to Shelly. I got down on the wall beside her. My hands couldn't even meet behind her. She grabbed me and locked her fingers at my back. Pulling. As if she was trying to pull herself right out of that miserable existence. I knew she'd been abused when she was young but now I could actually feel it. Nothing; not the smell of drink, nor the stink of tobacco, nor stale sweat, nor the waft of pish, could've stopped me giving her a cuddle. When I loosened my grip she held on tighter. I tried to let go but she squeezed.

—Don't let me go, she kept saying. —Don't let me go.

A tear came out of me then cos I knew there was no way she was ever going to break free. I decided to hold her for as long as it took. Bruce Springsteen would have to wait.

After a minute I heard Billy crying. Billy Brown. The best boxer in the west. A legend. Crying.

—What about me? he was saying. —What about me? I want a cuddle.

Shelly let me go.

—Give Billy a cuddle, she said, —Billy needs a cuddle.

He was over in the corner and his cheekbones were wet. I gave Joe a look as I passed him. I don't know if he ever knew what that look meant. But I tried to say – sometimes there's things in life you've got to do, Joe. Sometimes Joe, you've got to look over and beyond your prejudice and disgust and disappointment. Sometimes you've just got to love, Joe.

But I don't think he got all that.

I took Billy and held onto him. Man drowning at sea. Billy'd been sober a few times and we both knew what that meant. Some bit of him was trying to climb out. But it was all caving in. Tumbling.

—Everything's going to be all right Billy, I said, —everything's going to be all right.

But I knew, and Billy knew, and everybody up that close knew everything wasn't going to be alright. Everything was going to be far from alright. Billy pushed me away, looked in my eyes and said,

—You better get out of here big man. This close is no place for you.

—Don't you tell my brother what's good for him and what's not, Billy! Danny shouted.

—Don't hit him Billy, I whispered. —Not unless he hits you – then just do what's necessary.

Billy pulls a blade out. Waves it in the air making wee swishing noises by blowing air out of his mouth.

—I'll look after him Stevie, don't you worry.

Shelly starts shouting, —Billy's goanny kill them three bastards that chibbed Danny! Slash them to bits! Ain't ye Billy?

Billy looked me straight in the eye as he told her to shut her mouth. He kissed me on the cheek and everybody watched as I kissed him back. It was a moment of true love.

—Coming Joe? I said.

—Eh aye! He was and quick. Joe had that *what kind of a crazy place is this?* look on his face when we were walking out that close. Then a pique of guilt made me turn, go back in and thrust twenty quid in Danny's hand. He's going to get drink anyway and my figuring is the sooner he gets to where he can't take any more the better. Or maybe that's not it. Maybe that's me trying to moralise. To be the good guy. I think the truth of the twenty quid is more like this; I know what it's like to be choking for drink and have no money. Danny took the twenty and was crying. This time the tears were real. But they turned from despair to anxiety to anger to aggression and he went for me. Lunged in with a big haymaker of a punch. It was a postcard job. I could've made a cup of tea as I waited for it to come over. I dodged sideways. Billy held him back and Danny started ranting.

—Embarrassed to walk down the main street with your brother?

—What? I said.

—Embarrassed to walk down the main street with your brother?

—Nobody said nothing about walking down no main street Danny.

But he kept repeating himself so I said, —Come on then, we'll walk down to The Fountain and back.

He spat on me. That was his answer to that.

—I'm not walking down no fuckin main street so you can show off that you're sober! Oh look at me everybody! I've been off the drink for ninety years!

He swung a punch and hit the wall. Danced about sucking his knuckles.

—Look what you've made me do, he kept shouting. —Look what you've made me do!

There was no talking to him. I decided it would be best if I went. Joe was hanging about the edge not knowing to be embarrassed or not.

—I'm away, I said with no venom nor emotion that you could detect.

—See ye later, said Billy.

—Thanks for the cuddle, said Shelly. —Oh you've got lovely eyes by the way!

—It wasn't that when you were up this close with us ya prick! shouted Danny and ranted; bringing up the past.

—Shut up Danny! said Billy.

—He's an alky Joe – did ye know that about your Da? Eh? A dirty no good alky!

—Clamp it Danny, I'm warning ye! said Billy.

I was nearly back on main street when he shouted it.

—He killed a guy Joe, did ye know that?

Billy grabbed Danny but that didn't stop him.

—A punch. One punch Joe. He's a fuckin murderer.

Billy clamped his hand over Danny's mouth. But it was too late. The word echoed along the close and staggered out onto the street. People were walking in an arc round about it. Whether they knew it or not, they had heard it. And Joe had heard it. As I left the close I could hear their voices lessen. It reminded me of something I had read in a book about Romans. Echo was a nymph who was in love with Narcissus. But when he didn't love her back she pined away till only her voice remained. Only now I couldn't tell if it was Danny pining away or me.

Out on the main street the sun was shining and people came and went about their business. Joe sighed the way you do at a blinding movie. Like the opening scene of *Saving Private Ryan* or Rutger Hauer's speech on the roof in *Blade Runner*, or when Oedipus sticks thon pins in his eyes when the guilt for fuckin his mother finally hits home. And I was thinking about how easily we can pollute our whole family, our whole society, by the things we do, when Joe spoke.

—Come on Da, we'll go and get that CD, he said.

It was the first he'd ever called me Da. Joe never knew what I'd been in jail for but he never mentioned *murderer*. Not then and not since. We were lucky. We got the last copy of *The River* and I raved about it all the way back to the car. He got in just before me and I took a second to look at him and say a prayer or make a wish or whatever it is I do – that he'd not end up in the darkness of some close breaking his whole family's heart. We droove off and at The Fountain I could see, in the distance, the chinkee's close like a black hole in the brightness of the street. I watched it in my wing mirror till it disappeared into a dot and wondered if I'd ever see my brother again. Joe turned up the volume and The Boss sang loud and clear.

♫ Now those memories come back to haunt me, they haunt me like a curse. Is a dream a lie if it don't come true, or is it something worse, that sends me down to the river, though I know the river is dry...

As we droove with Joe playing air guitar a poem came into my head. The one about the donkey being the devil's living parody of all four-footed things. I identified with that donkey. Cos that's what we were. All of us. Fuckin donkeys. Steelwork or mine fodder. It gets its glory when it carries Jesus into Jerusalem – that ugly bastard of a donkey. That's all we ever done, guys like me and Billy and Danny and Shelly – waited for one moment of glory to transform our lives. Some kind of crazy epiphany. But looking round that town I could see clearly that the moments that transformed our lives were the ones that pulled us down. And once you hit rock bottom. You could stay there. Or you could climb.

## **Luath** Press Limited
*committed to publishing well written books worth reading*

LUATH PRESS takes its name from Robert Burns, whose little collie Luath (*Gael.*, swift or nimble) tripped up Jean Armour at a wedding and gave him the chance to speak to the woman who was to be his wife and the abiding love of his life. Burns called one of 'The Twa Dogs' Luath after Cuchullin's hunting dog in Ossian's *Fingal*. Luath Press was established in 1981 in the heart of Burns country, and is now based a few steps up the road from Burns' first lodgings on Edinburgh's Royal Mile.
Luath offers you distinctive writing with a hint of unexpected pleasures.

Most bookshops in the UK, the US, Canada, Australia, New Zealand and parts of Europe either carry our books in stock or can order them for you. To order direct from us, please send a £sterling cheque, postal order, international money order or your credit card details (number, address of cardholder and expiry date) to us at the address below. Please add post and packing as follows: UK – £1.00 per delivery address; overseas surface mail – £2.50 per delivery address; overseas air-mail – £3.50 for the first book to each delivery address, plus £1.00 for each addition-al book by airmail to the same address. If your order is a gift, we will happily enclose your card or message at no extra charge.

**Luath** Press Limited
543/2 Castlehill
The Royal Mile
Edinburgh EH1 2ND
Scotland
Telephone: 0131 225 4326 (24 hours)
Fax: 0131 225 4324
email: sales@luath.co.uk
Website: www.luath.co.uk